2020
THE ANIMAL UPRISING,
AND SO IT BEGINS

COLIN C EVANS

Ordering Information:

Prime Seven Media
518 Landmann St.
Tomah City, WI 54660

Printed in the United States of America

2020

The date is the 1ˢᵗ of March. The year is 2020.

And there have been some very strange things happening lately. Including some major changes being made to the order of power on this planet. And all these strange, unexplainable things, have happened just in these last couple of months. As every animal and insect on the planet appear to be losing their fear of mankind as urban foxes no longer ran away at the mere sight of a human.

And some have been known to brazenly walk into peoples' homes in the search of food and show no fear whatsoever when the people try to scare them out of their home. they have even been known to attack them. And these "strange things" have escalated beyond belief over the past few years. It's like living in a science fiction story.

The year is now 2030 and mankind have very little, if any, say on what happens on this planet. They are no longer the "superior beings" because the creatures of this world appear to have taken over.

For example, all oil drilling and seismic exploratory work in the Arctic Circle have been cancelled, "for the foreseeable future," due to the constant attacks on the workforce, twenty-four hours a day, seven days a week, by the polar bears and seabirds.

Even the normally placid seals and penguins, have been known to attack and on occasion kill, any unfriendly humans, that have been stupid enough to venture out onto the ice, for whatever reason.

The same sort of "strange things" have also started happening at sea, with the whales' dolphins, and seabirds attacking the fishing trawlers.

They managed to sink one Japanese "scientific research" whaling ship, when around forty whales, which were a mixture of blue whales, sperm whales, and even the smaller Minke whales, none of which have ever been known to attack humans in the wild were involved and are responsible for at least one hundred and thirty-eight deaths.

It also appears that these creatures, have somehow become "self-aware." Because, when any surviving CCTV film footage of these attacks was watched, it was obvious, even to the untrained eye, that these attacks were very well planned, and well executed, with every creature involved seeming to know exactly where to go, and what to do, and they moved like a well-trained army.

It was also noticed just how quickly these creatures could adapt to, and deal with any situation that arose. Now, there have been many varied, and some downright weird theories put forward, one person suggested it was an act of God, which didn't go down very well with his learned colleagues, another person suggested that it could well be the result of Genetic engineering, possibly caused by these creatures consuming plants that have been genetically modified.

And one theory came from a top human professor, who was also the person responsible for carrying out the spindle cell research. His name is James (Jimmy) Trew, (who was laughed at by his peers, for putting forward such a ridiculous notion,) because he suggested it was all down to the number of spindle cells in a creatures' DNA.

Now, spindle cells, are responsible for language, recognition, memory, and so on. Therefore, they play a very important part of intelligence.

(All humans have them in their DNA.) However, it has just been scientifically proven that magpies, and all members of the crow family, along with all species of whales, dolphins, elephants, and the great apes, have three times the amount of these spindle cells in their DNA than humans.

(This is a fact,) so, it would seem these animals are the most intelligent species on the planet, with humans claiming a very poor second, just in front of the rats, mice, cockroaches, and spiders.

Humanity has also been receiving reports from around the world, that various species of whales have been spotted congregating in large numbers, and it looks as if they have now joined forces.

They've also been making what appear to be meticulously planned, and well-orchestrated attacks on all commercial shipping, (the Japanese whaling ship for example.) The whales Have also been seen driving other fish away from any fishing trawlers that have been brave, (or stupid) enough, to put out to sea, so the fishermen have been running a very real risk of being attacked, and quite possibly sank.

The whales have also been seen protecting larger shoals of fish, by swimming around them in large numbers, thereby encircling them, in a living rotating wall, to keep them safe from the trawler's massive nets. So, the trawlers are going back to port empty handed, and have been doing so for the last few months.

The fishermen must now decide if it's worth risking their lives for nothing, because during these last couple of months, over one hundred and twenty trawlers have been destroyed, and many human lives have already been lost, and the numbers are still steadily rising.

But, these strange occurrences, are by no means unique to the oceans, because it's now happening all around the world, with elephants, rhinos, gorillas, and tigers, that apparently have now developed the ability to communicate with each other, and have now joined forces, attacking, and killing the poachers that have mercilessly persecuted them for so many years.

The Elephants have been ripping the bottom jaws out of the poachers, and then leaving them to slowly bleed to an agonizing death, just as the poachers do to them.

Even the shy and peaceful Orang Utangs, have been getting involved, and are responsible for at least eleven deaths in one area of rainforest alone, they have even used the poacher's own traps and snares to catch them, (as have the Mountain Gorillas.)

So now the poachers know exactly what it feels like to be caught in a painful trap, just waiting to die. Although, in many cases the loggers are burning the Orang Utangs to death, because for some reason they seem to class it as entertainment, (sadly, this is a fact.)

Now, humanity has not taken kindly to the change from hunter to hunted, or the fact that they have been removed from the number one spot, now that there's actual proof that mankind are not the superior beings after all, (which we have known for several centuries.)

One explanation put forward, by the same top human scientist that I mentioned earlier, Professor James (Jimmy) Trew, suggested that the creatures of this world, are now joining forces, because they have had enough of humanity's constant attempts to eradicate them all. All thanks to the human disease called greed. (This disease is merciless and can turn the nicest person into a ruthless tyrant withing a very short space of time. And is all consuming.)

And this goes hand in hand with man's constant need to destroy everything in his path, for his own gain, or a quick profit. With no regard whatsoever, for the consequences to either animal or human life. However, all professor Trew who made the remark, received from his esteemed colleagues, was insults and ridicule, for once again daring to insult their intelligence, by making such a ludicrous, and completely unproven so therefore, unfounded statement.

Even when professor Trew placed the scientific proof in front of them, in black and white, they still, point blankly, refused to accept it as fact, and it caused quite a few rather intense and heated arguments.

Now, while these discussions were going on, the animals and insects had been rather busy, getting themselves organized as more and more become "self-aware." They had been organizing raiding parties on the medical and cosmetic research laboratories all around the world, and releasing the creatures kept there; they even used some of the "not so friendly" researchers for a few experiments of their own, and quite literally gave them a taste of their own medicine, which I personally thought was hilarious.

They have also been busy liberating the zoos all around the world, and releasing the "inmates," many of which have been busy punishing humanity in various ways, ranging from alligators and crocodiles taking over people's swimming pools, and have been known to eat any family pets that didn't want to change and were happy to stay where they were, living as pampered pets.

Food supplies were being ransacked by hungry animals, and some people were killed in "freak accidents," caused by damaged brake hoses on their vehicles.

Many large open spaces, such as central park in America, along with many stately homes and palaces worldwide, including the queen's residence in London, Buckingham palace. Becoming officially classed as "no go areas" for humans, and many of these areas now have groups of heavily armed guards constantly patrolling, in order to protect people from the dangerous animals that now reside there.

But there are reports continually being made by the armed guards, that quite a few people are deliberately sneaking into the no-go areas and have been seen leaving food for the various creatures that now inhabit these places.

Plus, a few of the local villains have been known to throw the odd body or two over the walls, in the hope that the hungry animals would eat them, thereby disposing of the evidence, but the animals, just dragged them back out onto the road, and in plain view of the armed guards, who then contact the police.

And much to everyone's surprise, and contrary to the media reports, these dangerous animals haven't attacked any friendly people. Unlike the people who tried giving poisoned food to any animal that would accept it, and the same thing applies to the zookeepers, and other members of staff all over the world, because not a single one was hurt in any way, during the big escape.

Now, the reason for this was mainly out of respect and gratitude, because of the zoos worldwide breeding programmes, that have saved so many of these species from extinction. And, as I mentioned earlier, all of this has happened in the last ten years.

Now, it all started going "a bit weird," when for the first time in human history, the northern lights appeared, ever so briefly, over Trafalgar square in the Centre of London, this happened on the very last stroke of midnight on December the thirty-first 2019. Or, if you prefer, the very first stroke of New Year's Day 2020, It all depends on the way you want to look at it, because the last stroke signifies the end of one year, yet it also confirms the beginning of another. I suppose it's a bit of a glass half full or half-empty sort of thing.

On January the second, people started to notice how certain animals attitudes towards humans had changed, because urban foxes, and badgers, along with rats and mice, were now just casually walking straight in to people's homes, looking for food, somehow they had lost all fear of mankind, because when people tried to scare them off, these creatures would just stand there, and stare at them, for several minutes, they would then carry on with what they were doing, completely ignoring any attempts to scare them off.

As the weeks turned into months, every animal and insect in the world had gradually lost all fear of humanity, and they'd started gathering together in large numbers, attacking the people that had constantly abused them for years, especially the animals used for scientific, and cosmetic research.

Even household pets had started looking at their owners with a strange, knowing look in their eyes, as if to say don't you worry, I'm just biding my time. And many pet owners were now becoming very wary, or even frightened, of their once beloved pampered pets. many of which had been "disposed of" and some were just abandoned on the roadside.

But the strangest thing of all, is these creatures were not just randomly attacking, and or killing people, just for the sake of it. Despite what the official media, "animals go on a killing spree" reports may say. In fact, it's very much the opposite, as they seem to be one hundred percent focused, very well organized, and well regimented. They also seem to know exactly what they're doing, and where they're going, as if working to some sort of master plan, which the top human brains of the world (with hindsight,) have now decided, appears to be shutting down the artificial world that humanity has created for themselves.

This just goes to prove that Professor James, (Jimmy) Trew, was right all along, but of course, he has never received any sort of credit for his work, plus his peers, who really didn't appreciate him proving them all wrong, along with the public humiliation he put them through, now treat him with nothing but the utmost contempt.

And of course, so many different rumours are going around, about what the animals intend to do, which range from breeding people for food in factory farms, to turning the human race into slaves, or even keeping them as pets, which has driven humanity into responding in the usual way, with guns, poisons, and traps. Complete with the armed forces receiving the usual standard order, which of course is, if it moves, kill it, and ask questions later.

However, I don't believe humanity will find it as easy to regain power as they seem to think, and I know for a fact that there will be quite a few fundamental and life altering changes, made for the better in this world. Unfortunately, for them, these changes are not necessarily to the advantage of humanity, in fact very much the contrary, thanks to the realization that mankind are not, (or ever were) needed on this planet, as they are nothing more than irresponsible, greedy parasites, that seem incapable of using their so-called superior intelligence, to see that they are destroying everything they need to survive on this planet, regardless of the cost, in both human and animal lives. Humans are strange creatures, they worship a god they cannot see, yet they destroy the nature that they can see, without realizing they are the same thing. Nature is the Creator.

How can I be certain of these changes? Well, unfortunately, I can't reveal how, at this moment in time, simply because you would not accept what I say as the truth, honestly, you would not believe me, however, as a true soldier, I give you my word of honour, that I will explain everything in greater detail a little later on.

It also seems a strange coincidence that this all started in the year twenty-twenty, because it is also the number for perfect eyesight, because since these animals have become "self-aware," and have had their eyes opened, so to speak, to what mankind is doing to this planet, they seem to have a perfect vision of what must be done.

They also appear to be very determined to fulfil this vision, no matter what the cost, because so many things depend on them winning this war against humanity, that they are quite literally, willing to do whatever it takes.

They also appear to be evolving at a breathtakingly fast pace, because the organizational, and communication skills of these creatures, are rapidly improving, getting stronger and stronger by the hour, and it's now spreading like a plague, "infecting" every animal, and insect, on the entire planet.

And, according to some top animal behavioral experts, that have just spent the last two months, meticulously studying all the available film footage of these creatures during the various assaults, it has been indisputably proven, that these creatures, are also capable of talking to each other, and, according to these experts, they can even communicate with different species, anywhere in the world, whether it's an animal, or insect. For example, an ant in the United Kingdom can talk to an elephant in Africa.

Now, exactly how they've managed to do this, no one seems to know, although there have been quite a few suggestions put forward, such as telepathy, body language, similar to a bee, dancing, to tell the other bees the best place to go for flowers etc. Another suggestion put forward, was how they could be using pheromones, to create a universal language, similar to that used by a colony of ants.

Because these creatures, just like a colony of ants, now appear to have a "collective consciousness, and intelligence" (which is the correct answer) because by sharing information, these creatures increase their intelligence, and by sharing everything in their collective mind, it enables them to think ten times faster than mankind. (Although, mankind hasn't realized this yet.)

However, as these different theories are put forward, they just seem to raise even more unanswerable questions, such as, where did this language come from? What caused it to happen? And what's making these creatures act the way they are?

Now, no one has the answers to these questions, and try as they might to find the solution, after three years of concentrated effort, they finally had to concede that they knew nothing more than when they started, and many of the top officials of this world, are now becoming extremely paranoid about it.

They have also received reports of fire ants, bees, hornets, and wasps, combining forces, the fire ants, that are drawn instinctively by nature to the pulses emitting from the electrical supply, seem to be the ringleaders; and they have now taken over and disabled all the telecommunication systems worldwide, including every television, and radio station, along with all satellite and mobile phone masts, and of course all radar systems.

But, in all fairness, humanity did receive a warning before everything was shut down, stating that nothing would be allowed to take off from any airports, and all aircraft, including all RAF flights, should land as soon as possible, because the world's radar and navigational systems, would be turned off in a maximum of two hours, regardless of the consequences, and the same message was sent to the royal and merchant navy, along with all passenger carrying vessels.

Now, this announcement came as a complete shock to the top military officials, and they were quite taken aback by this move, because these "dumb creatures," had just implemented one of the first rules of warfare, which is to disable your opponents' communication and transport systems, thereby making all opposition extremely difficult.

Therefore, this "joining of minds," has forced everything on the entire planet to shut down, and they accomplished this feat with remarkable ease, because humanity had absolutely no idea of what was going on and were completely powerless to stop them. The governments of this world have all gone into a blind panic as they realise that all the power and authority they once had has now disappeared. Possibly forever.

However, the really frightening thing, is just how easily they made all of this happen, in just one day. These creatures appeared to be in complete control, of what, and where, anything happened.

You could even say, they appeared to be thoroughly enjoying themselves, as if thriving on the rush coming from a well-organized plan, as it comes to completion. So, humanity, now have no way of instantly communicating with each other over a distance, except for semaphore, this is what the navy used in the Second World War, which consists of waving flags in a certain order.

The only other method was using a flashing light for Morse code, but unfortunately for humanity, not many people know how to use, or more importantly, how to decipher, either of these archaic methods of communication.

Therefore, the only way humanity can talk to each other now, is either face-to-face, or by sending a human messenger, obviously, carrier pigeons can't be used, (although they did try,) and my, how we laughed, at just how stupid, gullible, and incredibly vulnerable humanity are without the all-important gadgets and technology, that they so desperately rely on, even for the simplest of tasks, because, as soon as these things were either destroyed or disabled, the entire fabric of human society disintegrated, as many people realized that without the technology used to run their mobile phones they were now pretty much incapable of thinking for themselves.

And just to make matters worse, people all over the world, are now beginning to ask their governments all sorts of awkward questions about what's going on, because there's been a global cover up, so as not to "create panic in the public".

So, the governments of this world have now been left with no other option, and they've been forced to come clean, simply because there's been so many unexplainably strange things happening, and not just here in the United Kingdom, but all over the world, as people's homes, schools, offices, and shops, became overrun by mice and rats, along with all manner of creepy crawly insects, and life for many humans has now become a living nightmare, from which it seems there is no escape.

The first place this "vermin" descended on in the United Kingdom, was the Centre of London. And it all started at eight forty-five precisely, on a busy Friday morning. And they arrived with a vengeance, as there were literally millions of them, and their numbers were still rapidly increasing.

And all unbeknown to the oblivious people above them, as they rushed around like the white rabbit from Alice in wonderland, in their constant hurry to get to their destination. Because the "vermin," had congregated in the huge network of sewers, that lie directly below the busy streets of London's city Centre.

And, when every last inch of the sewer was full to bursting point, eventually, the ancient pipework and tunnels, just through the sheer volume of them all, combined with the incredible back pressure, being created by the huge amount of backed up human waste, that had now started oozing out of a large number of toilets, both household and business alike, finally, the sewers could no longer contain them, something had to give.

And then it happened. The "vermin," still awaiting the command to attack, finally lost their tenuous grip on the ancient crumbling pipe work and tunnel walls, causing them to explode out of every manhole, drain (and quite a few toilets) like a volcanic eruption.

The surge from the suddenly released highly pressurised raw sewage, propelled a huge number of rats and mice, (along with some rather startled spiders,) as much as thirty feet, (ten metres) or more up into the air.

Many of the stunned and somewhat bewildered people, whose brains were now racing, frantically, as they struggled to find a logical answer to this unknown conundrum they were now facing, many thought that maybe the banks of the river Thames had burst its banks, because at first glance, it looked as if there was a flood of dirty brown water, rushing towards them.

But all that changed, as soon as the flying rats and mice started landing on, and attacking them, (plus human excrement,) and then they suddenly realized that this "flood," wasn't water at all, but a huge seething mass of angry and rapidly approaching vermin, and that's when mass panic, blind hysteria, along with mankind's inbuilt survival instinct, instantly took over.

An estimated five thousand people were injured, crushed, or killed, in the mayhem that followed; an estimated one hundred and seventy people, died instantly of heart attacks, brought on just by the sheer shock of it all. Many others were quite simply trampled to death by the huge number of stampeding people, as they desperately attempted to escape this terrifying deluge.

Others were quite simply mown down by cars, Lorries, and buses, as they fled blindly into the oncoming traffic, as they tried to escape the oncoming onslaught. Many drivers were killed as they blindly crashed into other vehicles at high speed, thereby instantly crushing them to death.

While, many other less fortunate people, died screaming in fear and agony, as they realized they were doomed to a slow painful death, as they sat trapped in their burning vehicles, unable to escape, knowing full well, that their incessant agony and fear induced screams for help, were falling on deaf ears, and no one was going to help them.

One trapped person, was on their mobile phone, (even though he knew the phone masts had been turned off) in an attempt to say goodbye to their loved ones, but had the phone snatched, and stolen, so he died not knowing if his message got through to his family. Some, were killed by trains, as they sought refuge in the underground rail systems, but to no avail, as the vermin were literally everywhere, and there was no way of escaping this horrific nightmare.

The rats and mice had flooded into every shop and office block; they then set about destroying every piece of equipment in these buildings. Some people were crushed by others landing on them, as they leapt out of their high-rise office block windows, completely panic-stricken, in a desperate attempt to escape this unstoppable torrent of vermin, that had suddenly descended on them from nowhere.

The police freely admitted they were powerless, and completely overwhelmed by the carnage that was unfolding before their very eyes, one high-ranking police officer named Charles (Charley) Flello, said it was like watching a scene from a horror film.

He also admitted how he was still struggling to come to terms with many of the things he had witnessed, especially the horrific demise of a young woman who was a nurse on her way to work. Who, unfortunately for her, had stopped, and was trying to help the many injured people that now littered the streets, her name, was Susan Hannon, and he had watched helplessly, as she was literally eaten alive by rats.

He later told reporters, how, as if in slow motion, he had watched two rats scurry up the young woman's legs, and start to eat their way into her, gnawing their way into the soft flesh of her stomach, until eventually re-emerging through the small of her back, one either side of her now visible spine. and thereby destroying some of her vital organs. Whilst others had followed them up into her stomach and had worked their way up through the young woman's chest cavity, feasting on the rest of her protein rich internal organs, while the unfortunate young woman was stood there, transfixed, with a mix of fear, shock, and total disbelief of what was happening to her. Her sky-blue eyes full of shock and horror.

She had stood there for what was no more than a few minutes at the most, but to her it must have felt like an eternity, as she stood there, completely motionless, like some sort of bizarre sculpture. Her mouth wide open, in a silent scream, except for a brief gush of air, like a deflating balloon, as the rats ate their way up through her lungs, before finally exiting her now lifeless body through her shoulders, as she slowly crumpled to the ground, her ordeal, thankfully, now over.

Now, quite a large number of people had been bitten or killed by the rats, but this unfortunate young woman was (thankfully) the only one to be eaten alive. And many of the human soldiers, were overheard admitting that they believed it to be nothing more than an "unfortunate accident," caused in the heat of the moment.

Because it looked as if the "vermin" were more interested in the actual buildings, and destroying its contents, than killing the unfortunate people who were unlucky enough to be in the premises when they arrived.

Because when the CCTV footage was eventually found and played back, it was noticed that several "teams" of rats and mice appeared to be attempting to usher these people out of the buildings, and they only fought back in self-defence.

Then the armed forces were ordered to respond, but there was very little, or nothing they could actually do. First of all, they were ordered to evacuate the Centre of London.

This took them three weeks to organize and complete, which wasn't bad going really, I suppose, considering they now had no way of instantly communicating with either their superiors, or the men under their command. Then, once the evacuation had been completed, the order was issued for them to go in, clean-up, and destroy any remaining rats or mice that were still in the premises.

However, as soon as the soldiers entered the buildings and started firing, they immediately realized that guns were not the right tools for the job, because they were causing too much damage to the buildings and its contents, and having very little, if any, effect on the intended targets.

Along with the fact that quite a few soldiers were accidentally shot by their own side, because thirty-seven soldiers died during a bout of erratic firing, as some of the newly trained soldiers became overwhelmed by the sheer numbers of vermin coming at them. And panic-stricken, they just started firing wildly and blindly at anything and everything that so much as made a sound or moved a muscle.

So, the order to retreat was immediately issued. The soldiers tried pumping poisonous gas into the buildings, but the rats and mice just retreated until the gas had cleared before going back into the buildings. Then, suddenly, as if from nowhere, three large army lorries appeared, between them they were carrying a total of six hundred flamethrowers, that were left over from the Second World War, the soldiers were ordered to strap them to their backs, they were given a quick lesson in how to use them then they were ordered to go back in for another go. And this time, they did manage to kill a few thousand rats and mice.

Which, at the time, seemed a bit odd to the soldiers, because although the buildings had appeared to be full of "vermin" on the first attempt to remove them, however, there didn't seem to be that many of them, if you know what I mean? The soldiers then realized that the "vermin" they had initially attacked with guns, were in fact, nothing more than a skeleton crew, that had since sent out for reinforcements.

So now the flamethrowers were not really having much of an effect on them, because the more the soldiers killed, the stronger they appeared to get, and the soldiers, who had been in the building for just over an hour, were now knee deep in burning, dead, or dying vermin, which also made any sort of movement extremely difficult. Plus, the air was full of smoke, along with the stomach-turning stench of burnt flesh along with the horrendous high-pitched agony induced squeals coming from the injured vermin. Many soldiers could be seen putting their hands over their ears in an attempt to drown out the ear-piercing sound, which of course left them defenceless, which the vermin were very quick to take advantage of and the soldiers were very quickly "dispatched."

This "vermin" had killed an estimated eighty-seven soldiers in the first thirty minutes of the attack, then for some unknown reason, everything just stopped, the vermin had somehow disappeared. A few moments later the bewildered soldiers suddenly realized why they'd disappeared, because there was a loud explosion, and approximately fifty soldiers, were unexplainably either instantly killed, burnt to death, or seriously injured by one of their own men. All of which was caused by a quiet, somewhat shy, and unobtrusive little field mouse whose name was Eolhc.

Because she had rather sneakily scurried up the leg of one of the soldiers and gnawed her way through the fuel pipe on the soldiers' flamethrower, which then sprayed the unfortunate soldier with a fine mist of fuel, thereby causing him to burst into flames.

And in his panic-stricken attempt to put himself out, he'd inadvertently ended up spraying quite a few of his own kind, so there were a few more loud explosions, as the fuel tanks on the injured or dead soldiers' flamethrowers blew up, thereby causing a chain reaction. And approximately two hundred soldiers were either killed or badly injured, so once again, the order to retreat was issued.

One soldier, a lieutenant named Dave Hedman, was overheard saying, to no one in particular, as they came out of the building, I can't believe we've just been beaten by a load of vermin, along with the fact that they made no attempt whatsoever to run away

In fact, it was very much the opposite, because when the soldiers had re-entered the building with the flamethrowers, the rats and mice were ready for them, eagerly awaiting their return, they were stood there, in a three-line formation, glaring back at them, their hackles up, squealing, and hissing so loudly at the soldiers that it hurt their ears, even puncturing some of the soldier's eardrums. These "vermin" were now more than willing to do battle, no longer afraid of mankind, and with a very determined look in their eyes.

So, once again, Lieutenant Dave Hedman asked what the hell's going on here, again to no one in particular, and once again, he received no reply, because his colleagues, many of which like him, were battle-hardened soldiers, were all as shocked and confused as he was, because nothing in their training, or their many years of service would ever have prepared them for this onslaught.

Another officer, named Kyle Lewis, who was the person in charge of this squad of soldiers that were helping in the clean-up operation, commented, we need some answers, and we need them now, so four messengers were immediately dispatched to H Q for more information, and hopefully, some answers.

So, while they waited in anticipation for the messengers return, (because they had lost quite a few) it was decided that the dead, and injured men, should be removed from the buildings, once the fires caused by the exploding flamethrowers had been put out.

Plus, the bulk of the dead and dying vermin that now stood just over a metre high throughout the building, had to be removed, so the medics could see the injured and dying men they needed to treat.

The rats and mice that had left the buildings just before the explosions, had also returned as soon as the fires had been extinguished. But this time, they kept a minimum of two metres away from the soldiers, that had already started removing most of the vermin's still smoldering corpses, that were now being piled high in the street, in full view of the general public, that were now becoming visibly reviled by what was in front of them.

Many of which were retching violently, as the putrid stench of burnt flesh suddenly reached their nostrils, as they attempted to walk past this ever-growing mountain of twitching, foul-smelling bodies, some of which were really badly burnt, but still very much alive, and squealing in agony.

Now, while this was in progress, the commanding officer, namely one Colonel Chris (Acey) James, commented on the fact that neither the rats, or the mice, attacked anyone that went into the buildings to retrieve the bodies, or to treat the injured and the dying where they lay. Instead, they were crouched, as if ready to spring, staring intently at the soldiers, watching every move they made.

Colonel Chris (Acey) James, also added, you had a very strange feeling come over you as you first entered the premises, because you could actually feel the tension in the air; yet it was more unnerving rather than frightening, if you know what I mean. Simply because of the overwhelming eerie silence, that literally hit you as you walked into the building.

Because you really could have heard a pin drop, (the badly injured soldiers were completely silent, and (thankfully) the rats high pitched squealing had also stopped. It was as if an uneasy, and unspoken truce, had somehow been called between both sides. And the soldiers strangely seemed to sense they would remain unharmed while the dead and injured soldiers were either removed from the building or treated where they lay.

So, just to prove this point, the little field mouse Eolhc, who was responsible for this carnage, had picked up a field dressing that a medic had unknowingly dropped. She then attempted to return it to him, as he knelt on a cleared section of the floor, trying to treat a rather badly burnt soldier.

But, as she stood beside him, with the dressing still in her mouth, she instantly saw the look of shock, and total disbelief, mixed with confusion and fear, on the medic's face, especially when Eolhc placed the dressing on the floor directly in front of him, then, looking straight into his eyes, she spoke to the medic, and introduced herself to him, because she so desperately wanted to explain to him why all this was happening.

However, she knew, just by the look on his now ashen face, that if she so much as uttered one more word, the poor medic would have either ran from the building screaming, thinking he'd lost his mind, or quite probably died there and then, of a massive heart attack.

Eolhc could see him visibly shaking uncontrollably, and the poor medic looked as if he were about to go into shock at any moment, so Eolhc had no other choice, she just left the field dressing on the floor, next to the medic, then quickly turning around and scurrying back to her friends. All of which had been intently watching her every move, in case she was attacked, because she was now a hero. And unbeknown to her, was destined to hold one of the highest ranks in the organization.

So, later in the evening, the medic decided that he had to go and tell his commanding officer, Colonel Chris (Acey) James, his incredible story of the talking field mouse, not thinking for one moment that the officer would believe a single word he said.

However, he really didn't care if the officer believed him or not, because he just had to tell someone before it drove him insane. The story ended with, and I quote, the medic's exact words were.

I am not proud to admit this sir, although I must say beforehand, I was more shocked and surprised rather than frightened, but I lost all control of my bowels, sir, and I quite literally shit myself.

I know just how crazy it all sounds, but how often do you meet a friendly, talking, well spoken, and seemingly highly intelligent field mouse. Not to mention the very strange circumstances all of this has happened under, unbelievable? Isn't it just?

Not to mention all the other strange things that are going on, so you can believe me when I say, scary is very much an understatement. The medic didn't know that Colonel James had witnessed the strange sight of a little mouse with a field dressing in its mouth, heading towards the medic, but he had then been distracted by one of his men, requesting permission to start removing the dead soldiers from the building. So, the officer had gone into another room, to get things organized, and hadn't seen what had happened.

So, and much to the medic's surprise, Colonel James did believe the story, and quickly swore the medic whose name was Craig Orton to secrecy. He was also ordered not to repeat so much as a single word of his story to another living soul.

To which the medic replied (with a rather surprised and bewildered tone to his voice) there's no one I could tell sir. The badly burnt soldier that I was treating at the time, who was also my only witness, has died of his injuries. Plus, no one in their right mind would ever believe such a story, unless, like yourself, they had seen it with their own eyes.

I know I wouldn't believe such a story. And if I did tell anyone, then I dare say they would more than likely put me in the nut house, and throw away the key, or worse, I'd go missing in action.

And there the story of this incredible, (but so far fictitious,) talking mouse should have ended. Unfortunately for Eolhc, it was just the beginning of what would become a massive nationwide search for her, and all because the medic's commanding officer, was convinced that this incredible story of a talking mouse was true.

So, he, in turn, retold the story to his commanding officer, and that person was a Colonel Glyn Adams. He was also the person in charge of resolving this "invasion of vermin" problem.

Now I've been reliably informed that Colonel Adams is a firm, but fair man, and is highly respected by both work colleagues and friends alike. Unfortunately, as of yet I haven't had the pleasure of making his acquaintance, although I am fairly certain that this will be rectified, hopefully in the not-too-distant future.

So, the medic, along with Colonel Chris (Acey) James, was ordered to attend a meeting with Colonel Glyn Adams at his office, which is situated in Builth Wells in South Wales. And the meeting appeared to be going quite well, or should I say, it was going quite well, until the medic was asked by Colonel Adams to give a description of this so-called talking mouse. Because all the medic could say to the Colonel was, Phhfff, no offence sir, but a mouse is a mouse, they all look the same, don't they? This was quickly followed by a very nervous laugh, that made the medic sound like a lunatic. (Much to the dismay of Colonel James.)

So, the medic was rather sternly dismissed, and told to return immediately to his duties, by a very unhappy, and still very sceptical Colonel Adams, who didn't take too kindly to people wasting his valuable time or trying to make a fool out of him.

So, once again, that should have been the end of it. However, a few days later, the medic suddenly remembered seeing a small white mark, on the back of the mouse's right ear, he had noticed this white mark as she'd scurried away from him, after returning the field dressing.

So, he quickly went and told his commanding officer what he had remembered, and once again, he was ordered to attend a meeting, where he told Colonel Adams exactly what he'd told his commanding officer. (This time without the maniacal laugh.)

And after a little bit of coaxing from Colonel Chris James, a description of the mouse was sent out to every army, air force, and naval base in the country. Along with a strict order, that at all costs, this little field mouse must be captured alive, and no matter what the circumstances it must not be harmed in any way.

Much to the amusement of the soldiers, sailors, and pilots, who instantly started making jokes about it, and came out with little quips such as, ah okay then, so this little mouse must obviously be one of the big cheeses, that keep the wheels turning, and one of the ringleaders.

However, it also made their job of eradicating the vermin that had taken over London practically impossible, so most of the time the soldiers were just sat around, half-heartedly watching the rats and mice as they scurried around, whilst they pretended to be looking for this little White mark.

Although, I dare say, they would have tried a lot harder, if they had known just how close to the truth those jokes were, because Eolhc. had become a very important, highly valued, and highly respected member of this organization, which are now known as the F T W, because at the moment she was one of the few creatures that could talk verbally to people.

Word soon got back to the F T W, which is now known to stand for Free This World, about what was being planned, and over the next few weeks' seventeen mice with small white marks behind their ears, were caught in various locations across the entire country.

Which the soldiers later, (much to their dismay,) discovered to be nothing more than white paint, or tipex, that had been deliberately placed there, to throw them off the scent, so to speak.

Much to the annoyance of Colonel Adams, who just could not believe that not a single one of the soldiers had the foresight, or the intelligence, to check the marking on the ear. (Some were even on the wrong ear) and much to the amusement of the F T W, who were now finding it highly amusing, (not to mention extremely easy,) to throw a spanner into the military works.

Unfortunately, Eolhc, was eventually captured, by a soldier who was busily washing an officer's car. He had spotted her as she tried to sneak past him, and he'd trapped her by placing an upturned bucket over her.

Yet, despite a very thorough search, and quite a few undercover reconnaissance trips all over the country, the F T W couldn't find any sign of her anywhere, much to the horror of the remaining leaders, and after two weeks with no word of her whereabouts, it was decided by some, but by no means all, that Eolhc must be dead.

Thankfully, many of her friends and supporters refused to give up hope and continued to search for her. Then, halfway through the third week, it was discovered that she was still alive, and being held in a medical research laboratory in Merthyr Tydfil in South Wales.

How did they discover where she was? Well, unbelievably, one of the human researchers had told a fly that had landed on the canteen wall next to a table where he and his colleague were sitting. (In an attempt to listen in on their conversation,) and the researcher (whilst looking directly at the fly) also told it that the F T W now had quite a few human supporters, that would be more than willing to work undercover for them, and how they would be happy to help in any way they could.

This of course, came as a complete surprise to the F T W, because they had been so busy organizing and planning everything, that no one "picked up" on it. plus, I don't believe for one minute they ever considered the possibility of humans ever supporting them in any way whatsoever.

Although, at the moment, the F T W had a lot more important things on their mind, because a plan of action was needed to get Eolhc out of there, and it was needed urgently, because the F T W had it on good authority that she was being mercilessly tortured, in an attempt to get her to talk. Because the same fly had decided to go and look for her, the fly, had spotted her through a grill, in the ventilation ducting.

Yet, despite numerous attempts, in which many of her supporters died, they could not get anywhere near her, and fair play to Eolhc, she had not uttered a single word. Not even after two and a half weeks of constant torture. And now, Colonel Adams, was beginning to have second thoughts about the medic's story.

He was also now seriously beginning to doubt her ability to speak, because throughout her torture, she hadn't made a single sound, not even a squeak or squeal of pain. This was also the concluding factor in his decision that Eolhc was in fact incapable of making any sound whatsoever. Along with the fact they had repeatedly told her that if she spoke to them, they would immediately stop torturing her, they also promised they would release her.

So, after much thought, followed by a lengthy discussion with a colleague, who was also a good friend of his, a Colonel Toby Fry, Colonel Adams, finally decided to cut his losses and call it a day.

However, he had also decided that she had to die, just in case there was even the slightest element of truth in the story, plus there wasn't much hope of her recovering from the terrible injuries they had inflicted upon her little body. And much to the surprise of the guards,

Colonel Adams decided to do the deed himself, as he wanted to make sure her death was both quick, and clean, because as far as he was concerned, she had suffered enough.

He was also now convinced that ordering the hunt for a talking mouse, had been the biggest mistake he had ever made in his long and so far, unblemished career, because he now firmly believed Eolhc couldn't make any sound at all, let alone talk. Although, he would never admit that he'd made a mistake to the men under his command, he did however, (for some unknown reason) feel compelled to admit it to Eolhc.

And while he was telling her how sorry he was for causing her so much pain, and how it would all soon be over, as he intended to put an end to her misery, he had the strangest feeling that she was listening intently to every word he spoke, and she had a strange," knowing," sort of look about her.

Not one of fear, or even hatred, but more a look of understanding, and possibly, just a hint of pity in her eyes.

And now she was well aware of what was about to happen to her, and she wished he would stop talking, and just get on with it, and kill her, as it would be such a relief to end the agony, she was suffering due to the horrific injuries they had inflicted upon her during her torture.

It was all she could do to stop herself screaming at him and begging him to kill her. But she was still wise and conscious enough to know that if she uttered so much as a single word then the pain would never end.

Finally, after what seemed to be an eternity, the Colonel stopped talking, and as the butt of the rifle he was holding came hurtling downwards towards her, and just a split second before it hit her, she had one last surprise in store for Colonel Adams, just to prove him wrong, and to quite literally have the last word.

Because at that point, she screamed out as loudly as her pain riddled little voice would allow. My name is Eolhc. And then, it was finally over, and the excruciating pain had thankfully ended.

The Colonel, completely stunned by it all, just stood there, filled with shock, respect, and even a little sympathy, for this brave little creature, whose life he had just taken, and there was a little dampness around his eyes.

The shock was because he was absolutely convinced that the story had to be untrue, respect, stems from her bravery, and her courage, for not revealing anything, not even under the prolonged intense torture, that no human being could have endured.

And regret that he'd killed her, because he now had an overwhelming feeling, strange as this may sound, that if he had sat down and spoken to her as an equal, instead of torturing her, then things would have been very different indeed. And now he didn't see her as a little field mouse, but more of a worthy opponent.

Unfortunately, it was now too late, so the Colonel placed what was left of her battered and crushed little body, into a small wooden cigar box, and sealed it; he then took his lock knife from his pocket, and roughly carved the letters F T W into the lid.

Which he then placed just outside the main gate of the research Centre, with strict orders being given to the soldiers on gate duty, that it had to be left where it was, they were also ordered to turn a "blind eye," to any animal that may come to collect the box, and how it must be allowed to take it, so her own kind could take her, and give her the funeral she so rightly deserved.

And sure enough, later that evening at 23.00 hours, a young fox just strolled casually up to the main gate, walking directly below the huge floodlights, in full view of everyone, and making no attempt whatsoever to conceal its approach.

The fox very gently placed the box in its mouth, but then, instead of running off, it just stood there, in full view of the soldiers as it stood directly below the huge floodlights that towered above it, it was staring directly at them as they watched him through the window of their sentry box, until eventually they just had to raise their hand in a gesture of acknowledgement of its presence.

At which point, the fox, (whilst never taking his eyes off the soldiers,) slowly bowed its head briefly, as if to say thank you for returning Eolhc to them, then turning slowly, it walked away, until eventually disappearing into the night.

The soldiers told everyone they met the next day all about the fox, and its strange antics. And that's how little Eolhc became a hero, and a great inspiration to both man and animal alike, not bad going for a shy, inconspicuous little field mouse.

Thankfully, mankind had absolutely no idea of just how important this little field mouse had been to the F T W, if they had, then they could have quite easily reclaimed (although only temporarily,) their position as number one.

So, things were a little on the quiet side for a few months, and humanity once again began to arrogantly believe they were invincible, and that this strange phenomenon had ended as quickly as it had begun, as everything was now slowly but surely, getting back to some sort of normality.

When suddenly out of the blue, it all started again, but this time it was with extremely well-organized attacks by various insects on the oil refineries. Plus, hundreds of rabbits, badgers, moles, and foxes, had been busily digging huge networks of burrows, directly below the heavy land-based oil pipes, thereby causing the ground to collapse, fracturing and in many cases shattering the oil carrying pipes, and of course, they had also done the same to the gas and water pipes.

In the meantime, seabirds, and huge swarms of flies, mosquitoes, and all manner of other flying insects, were attacking the skeleton crews that were still working on the oil rigs. And while this was going on, large groups of whales, basking sharks, giant squid, octopuses, and huge shoals of fish, were now attacking, and in many cases buckling the huge supporting legs, causing irreparable damage, and occasionally even managing to topple a few of the drilling rigs.

Meanwhile, badgers, foxes, stoats, and weasels, along with various other animals including various birds of prey were busy taking over the power stations, and all of this was happening worldwide, and again all on the same day, and at the same time, which was at 04.30 GMT precisely.

And mankind didn't stand a chance against this onslaught. because now, it was personal, Killing Eolhc was the worst thing mankind could have done. And it could have quite easily escalated into a full on, no holds barred, war, that the F T W were determined to win.

Because, if they didn't stop mankind in their tracks, then there would be no future for them, or the planet. However, and fortunately for humanity, the F T W weren't as callous or as heartless as them, because they had no desire whatsoever to hurt, or to kill anyone. (Which is what allowed this problem to start, and to escalate into the major threat it has now become.)

So, it was decided the F T W would keep to the original plan. And they had already arranged and put into place one major approach. They were also very clever, and somewhat cunning, and devious, in their methods. Because the insects had now stopped going to any plants or crops belonging to humanity, including the genetically modified ones, especially the ones they'd purposely bred to kill the insects, regardless of whether it was a pollinator or predator.

And of course, because the insects were no longer pollinating the crops, they were rapidly dying, adding even more to humanity's confusion and frustration. Because they now had yet another problem to add to their ever-expanding list to contend with, along with how to keep warm, communication, somewhere safe to sleep, what they were going to eat, and where to get clean drinking water. because they had lost the majority of their homes, hotels, shops, and offices to the rats and mice. And mankind has finally realized that this was now a battle for their way of life, and possibly their very survival. (they had also now learnt just how crucial the insects were to the survival of all life on this planet because without them everything including humanity dies.)

Plus, they were very rapidly losing ground to the so-called "dumb animals and vermin," that they had taken so much for granted in the past, never giving so much as a second thought to how they treated them, or the physical and mental abuse inflicted upon them, in the name of work, sport, entertainment, science, and experimental use.

And with that thought in mind, humanity had been getting off quite lightly for a very long time. Fortunately, that is all beginning to change, as the tables have been turned, and mankind is now learning the hard way exactly how it feels to be thought of as nothing more than a nuisance, or a disposable commodity.

Because until recently, most of the human deaths had happened, either by accident, or in self-defence, many were caused by the people themselves, as they ran around like headless chickens as blind panic took over. But all of that could quite easily change very much for the worse, if mankind doesn't quickly realize, and understand what's really going on around them.

Because the longer they take coming to terms with the reality of what was happening, then the worse it would get. It's not really looking too good for humanity at the moment. London has practically ground to a halt, and it is now commonplace to see lions hunting gazelles in Hyde Park and on the gardens of Buckingham palace. (Along with all the other creatures that were released by the F T W from London Zoo.) So, London now resembles the plains of the Serengeti.

Every major city and large town in the world have been badly affected by the loss of all telecommunications, including the internet, plus near enough all its gas, water, sewage, and electricity supplies. Except for the energy produced by renewable resources, such as solar panels, the wind, and water turbines, which have remained completely untouched, except for the ones that have been ransacked by human looters.

So, mankind now has practically no means of communication, nowhere to live, no fuel or food, no heating, very little water, no sewage system, and of course no money. Because since the electricity had been shut down, the banks safes, all of which are fitted with high security electrically powered time locks, can't be opened, along with the fact that there's nothing left to spend the money on anyway.

Nevertheless of course, you still have people who are obsessed with money, and some still staunchly believe it will solve all of their problems, so they are now trying their hardest to break into the closed and unguarded banks, to steal its now worthless contents.

Because in reality, the money isn't worth the paper it's written on, and its only value now would be in helping to start a fire, in order to keep themselves warm.

Humanity has also taken to squabbling amongst themselves, as people are now starting to hoard what little food, water, fuel, and weapons they discover. Gangs of vigilantes have been formed, and they're sending out raiding parties in order to replenish their rapidly dwindling supplies, many of these gangs have now joined forces, becoming small, yet formidable armies, thereby giving them the capability to expand, and protect their territory and their interests from intruders, as anarchy finally sets in. Which to be honest, was inevitable, due to man's instinctively greedy nature.

Things haven't exactly been quiet at sea either, thanks to the large pods of whales, dolphins and even sharks of varying species, including the peaceful basking shark, are now involved in the blocking of entrances to every important port in the world. They are letting vessels enter, but absolutely nothing's being let out, and any that manage to break through this living blockade, is very quickly dealt with, and are given this choice, turn back, or we will sink you. And they have already proven on several occasions that they mean business.

All the oil and gas rigs out at sea have now been shut down completely. Many of which are now beyond repair, thanks to the constant attacks by the whales and sharks that I mentioned earlier. Along with the thousands of seabirds and flying insects, that have been simultaneously attacking from above, and taking them over.

Although as usual, they are letting the rescue helicopters and boats that were given clearance from the F T W access, to remove the unfortunate people, that were working on these rigs.

And thankfully, at long last, humanity has finally begun to realize, that as long as they don't launch any kind of attack on any of these creatures, then all the "captured" people would be released, completely unharmed.

And the same sort of thing has been happening on land, because every civilian airport in the world, has come to a complete standstill, except for the flights that had already been sanctioned by the F T W.

The military airfields and naval ports appear to be the main priority, because not one of them has managed to remain open, or fully functional, anywhere in the world.

The military guard dogs, horses, and animal mascots have now turned on their handlers and riders. Refusing to work, or let any human anywhere near them, many of the guard dogs have either escaped, or been released from their compounds and kennels, and are now doing patrols of their own.

However, this time, they are in packs of up to forty strong and are a very formidable force to be reckoned with. Plus, their numbers are rapidly increasing on a daily basis, thanks to the huge numbers of evicted household pets, wanting to join them, and are definitely no longer thought of as man's best friend.

Many of them have been thrown out, and abandoned, because the owners were too scared to have them anywhere near them, just in case the once beloved pet decided to turn on them.

So, mankind has now become completely paranoid, and are slowly, but surely, turning back into the basic animal they have always been. And man has finally realized, that without their all-important gadgets, and high technology, they are pretty much useless, defenceless, and extremely vulnerable, as they were now being forced to come to terms with the fact that they were not only fighting for their way of life, but also the very survival of their species.

Nevertheless, mankind is of course its own worst enemy, as many people saw this chaos as a golden opportunity to claim land and buildings. Because everyone else was so busy looking after "number one," and fighting amongst themselves over whatever scraps of food or fuel they come across, that no one took any notice of, or even cared about what these people were doing, just as long as those people didn't have something they wanted. Because then, it would have been a very different story indeed.

No one had really noticed, thanks to the manmade mayhem, that the organized attacks from the F T W had practically stopped, simply because humanity was now doing the job for them. And were just too busy killing each other to notice the drop in these attacks.

Because every rule and law that ever existed, anywhere in the world, is no longer valid, as the human race has now gone into complete and utter chaos, and the only law people recognize now is this, whoever has the biggest gun, or the biggest gang, can do whatever they want.

So, mass murder, rape, looting, and destruction of property is now becoming, and even more frighteningly, being accepted, as the norm. And the F T W were very tempted indeed to just sit back and enjoy the show, as mankind do what they do best, which is to destroy themselves.

But luckily for mankind, the F T W had concluded, that there was no way they could be as heartless as them, so it was decided (rather reluctantly by some) that sooner or later, the F T W would have to step in, and offer to help mankind find a solution, and to help them regain some sort of law and order over their species.

The year is now 2036, the human world is in complete and utter turmoil, and they have finally come to terms with the fact that this is the way things are going to be, unless they can somehow regain order amongst themselves, which wouldn't be an easy task by any means.

They have also exhausted all existing fuel reserves and are finally realizing that they can no longer use any kind of fossil fuels, and will have to rely solely on renewable energy, such as solar panels, wind, water turbines and hydrogen cells.

So, they are now concentrating on speeding up the production process, with the aim of increasing the number of them being used, (once they've repaired the factories that produced them) as many of them were ransacked, and pretty much destroyed by human looters.

As I said, things were fairly quiet for the F T W, most of the attacks made by them had practically stopped, except for the odd skirmish with looters and vigilantes, attempting to infiltrate some of the F T W headquarters.

One of which was situated in the show caves in a place called Neath, in South Wales, where looters had made a feeble attempt to steal whatever they could get their hands on. There were also a few concentrated attempts made to overthrow the F T W, all of which of course, failed miserably.

However, there was one thing that was being kept a very closely guarded secret from the general public, and that was the secret meeting being planned between the top human, and animal leaders from all around the world.

(The F T W agreeing to allow a few crucial flights from airports worldwide,) each flight would depart at different times, because without radar, the pilots would be flying by compass. And after a lengthy discussion between the F T W leaders, it was decided that the mountain gorillas should act as ambassadors, mainly because of their human-like appearance, along with the fact they are mankind's closest living relative.

One of the F T W ambassadors who volunteered to attend this meeting, was a knowledgeable young mountain gorilla named Yikem Snave, who unbeknown to the human leaders was the son of Haras Snave (an important member and matriarch of the group.) He was also the only grandson of one of the main leaders of the F T W whose name is Ycnan Snave. Now, neither Ycnan, nor Haras, wanted Yikem to represent the F T W at this meeting, mainly out of concern for his safety.

Because of the possible consequences if the human representatives discovered who he was, (if captured he could then be used as a bargaining tool,) but Yikem insisted on going, and nothing could deter him. This meeting was due to take place in a secret underground nuclear fallout shelter, situated in the mountain area of Colonel Glyn Adams hometown of Builth Wells, in South Wales.

The F T W had the area completely, and very discreetly, secured fourteen days before this meeting was due to take place just in case anything "unfortunate" had been planned for Yikem Snave, or any of his entourage.

The human security people arrived just two days before the meeting, and they didn't appear to be particularly concerned about searching for any possible security risks. (So, man still hasn't lost his cockiness) and some of them were still (naively) under the impression they were still in charge of everything.

They didn't even notice that the F T W were all around the place like a nasty rash and were listening intently to every word they said.

Now, all the questions that were going to be asked at this meeting, were presented to the "opposition" one week before the meeting was due to take place, so that (in theory) each side would know what to expect.

However, and more importantly to the F T W, this meant they would not have to speak, (unless it was absolutely necessary) because they could answer the questions using sign language, although they knew full well the humans would do their utmost to goad them into saying something, so they would know which ones to target for future reference.

The day of the meeting finally arrives, with dignitaries from both sides arriving on the same planes and helicopters.

Which resulted in a very quiet, and somewhat uneasy journey for most of the humans, although, there were several attempts made to "break the ice" by them attempting to engage the F T W in conversation, which only resulted in the humans receiving an "evil eye" glare, which was quickly accompanied by a low rumbling guttural growl as a response.

So, the humans quickly gave up on that idea, much to the amusement of Yikem and his entourage, who now took to growling at every human, that so much as gave them a sideways glance, and laughed inwardly at the verbal response of the people on the receiving end of these growls and grimaces.

However, the humans, even though they had been told in advance that some, if not all, of these creatures could not only speak, and obviously understand the English language, they were still sat well within earshot of Yikem and company, and were quite openly discussing amongst themselves, what possible solutions were to be put forward at this meeting.

One of them said we ought to put them all in the local zoo where they belong.

Another one of them even suggested putting Yikem and his companions against a wall, and shooting the lot of them, he then stated how their heads would look nice on the office wall, as they would make a nice talking point. And he was staring directly at Yikem as he said it, in an attempt to goad him, or any of his companions into making a verbal response.

Which, of course never came, because Yikem along with the other ambassadors were just sat there, looking all innocent, as if they didn't have the vaguest idea of what these humans were saying, because Yikem and company were under very strict orders on how they were not to talk to anyone, no matter what the circumstances.

Now, as I mentioned earlier, about the universal language theory being the correct answer, but mankind still hasn't figured that one out yet. (And I don't think anyone's in any particular rush to point it out to them) or the fact that not only can all animals and insects talk to each other verbally, but they can also talk to any other animal, or insect, anywhere in the world, almost telepathically. Thanks to the use of something very similar to pheromones, whether it's a single individual or a group, even a group of various species, and again I give you my word of honour, that I will reveal exactly how this all came about a little later.

Eventually, everyone arrives at the drop-off point, which was by the lake on the Brecon Beacons, (also known as the Black mountains,) in South Wales, then after a short helicopter ride, they eventually arrived at the nuclear fallout shelter in Builth Wells, where they were promptly ushered into the building, just in case any "prying eyes," were watching.

And once they were all safely inside, everyone was issued with a name badge to pin on their clothing, which of course Yikem and company couldn't use. So, they just threw them on the table, followed by a growl of contempt, at these so-called superior beings, for not having the intelligence to realize that mountain gorillas do not wear clothes.

And once they had all been shown to their seats by some rather nervous, and very apologetic humans, who constantly kept saying sorry to the F T W ambassadors, for the name badge cock up, much to the annoyance of Yikem, and his associates. So, this time, the humans received a very real "evil eye" and growl response for their trouble.

So, the aides quickly decided that it would be a very good idea to quit while they were ahead so to speak, and promptly retreated to the relative safety of the other side of the meeting room doors, much to the amusement of Yikem and his associates. And very much to the annoyance of Colonel Adams who was, after all, a professional soldier, and didn't take kindly to bearing the brunt of his men's mistakes.

And eventually, after many introductions, and long-winded diplomatic speeches from the humans, the meeting finally gets underway. Firstly, the human offered a deal, which in a nutshell, was for the F T W to hand full control of everything back over to them, and in return, the humans promised there would be no reprisals whatsoever, and everything would return to exactly how it was before.

Which obviously, didn't go down to well, because unbeknown to the humans, every single animal, and insect on the planet, was listening intently to this conversation, the F T W just sat like statues in their chairs, staring intently at the spokesman, not believing he had the nerve to say what he'd just said.

Then, suddenly, after a brief, and somewhat uncomfortable silence, the human representative that made the comment received an answer that no one, especially the F T W had expected, with Yikem letting out a blood-curdling growl, whilst (with surprising speed and agility) jumping over the table and lifting the person who had made the ludicrous comment, of his chair, and off the floor by the throat.

Yikem, then slammed him several times into the wall behind him with such a force that the human received a nasty gash to the back of his head and concussion, several broken ribs, was severely winded, so much so that he had great difficulty in breathing, (plus the broken ribs didn't help.)

He then received a very severe shaking from Yikem; eventually after a few minutes, (that must have seemed like a lifetime to the aide,), he was unceremoniously thrown into a corner of the room like a discarded toy by an angry child, for his audacity.

Not one of Yikem's entourage moved so much as a muscle, they just sat there, their eyes scanning the room, watching the other humans intently, just waiting, some even hoping for some sort of a response, which luckily for the humans, never came, as thankfully they had all frozen solid with a combination of surprise and fear.

So. Yikem walked around the table he had just jumped over, and sat back down in his chair, staring intently into Colonel Adams eyes as he made the short journey. As if to say, well, do you have any other smart arse remarks you'd like to make?

However, the Colonel looked away, just as the poor bloke who had received the shaking had eventually managed (rather unsteadily,) to get back on his feet, and had made it back to his seat, whilst keeping his gaze firmly fixed on the floor, to avoid accidentally making eye contact with Yikem. He then, (again rather shakily,) went to sit back in his chair, but he paused, just for a moment, and he had a rather thoughtful look on his face.

He then tried, (but failed dismally), to whisper very quietly to one of his colleague's. However, what he was asking, (a little bit louder than he intended,) was, could you please go and get me some clean underwear, as I appear to have soiled these ones.

However, and most unfortunately for him, Yikem and associates had also quite clearly heard his comment and laughed as loudly as they could at his predicament. Which of course just embarrassed the human representative even more, (if that was at all possible,) and all this conversation was sent "telepathically" all around the world, much to the amusement of the creatures who were listening intently. However, quite a few of the F T W officials were most definitely, not impressed by Yikem's actions, and he was told quite sternly by Ycnan and Haras Snave to stop acting like a human, and to behave himself. They were both now quite concerned about possible repercussions, however, after several awkward minutes, the aide finally returned, and discreetly as he possibly could, (because every pair of eyes in the room both human and animal, seemed to be mesmerized by his actions, and was watching his every move,) handed (as discreetly as he could) the unfortunate person the clean underwear. The representative, who had remained standing by his seat for what seemed to him to be forever, then went off rather sheepishly to the toilet, to do what he had to do.

When he returned to the still eerily silent table, he very nervously, whilst keeping his gaze fixed firmly on the floor, started to approach Yikem, and attempted to apologize for insulting his obvious intelligence, and for treating him and his colleagues like dumb animals. (Which of course went down like a lead balloon,) and he then looked up, looking Yikem straight in the eye, and while still walking forward held his hand out for Yikem to shake, as a form of an apology, to which Yikem just glared at him. But this time, the "evil eye" and the low guttural growl that accompanied it was very seriously meant indeed.

It was enough to stop the man dead in his tracks. And that's when the human representative realized that hell would freeze over, long before that hand would ever be shaken by Yikem or come to that any other F T W ambassador.

The person responsible for again embarrassing himself also received the evil eye from his superior officer, namely Colonel Glyn Adams, and I must admit that I still don't know to this day, which stare frightened him the most, and at one point, everyone in the room thought he was going to ask for some more underwear.

Yikem did not take kindly to pompous arrogant humans, who still refuse to acknowledge they are no longer, (or indeed ever have been,) the superior beings on this planet, and are not in charge of anything, which now also included their own future? So now the humans knew, in no uncertain terms, what they were dealing with. And that the F T W would not be messed around or pawned off with some empty promises and shiny trinkets, like the American Indian and the Mayan tribe's people. (No offence meant) That's when the humans realized they had to be completely honest, and upfront, about everything they had to say or offer.

So, questions were asked, and offers were made to the F T W that wasn't on the original list of questions, which made things quite difficult and somewhat awkward for a few hours. Because although the humans knew the F T W ambassadors could use sign language, they had somehow "forgotten" to have a human representative that could also use sign language, maybe it was all part of a well-planned ploy to get the F T W to speak. Then, after another long-drawn-out silent hour, Yikem "telepathically" asked his grandmother for permission to speak, which was promptly refused, however, permission was granted for one of his entourage to speak on his behalf. This spokesperson was a young female mountain gorilla named Eigroeg Snave, who was a last-minute replacement, quite simply because one of the original F T W representatives had literally dropped dead on the airport runway, as they were about to board the plane.

And she just happened to be there, (which will be explained shortly,) now Eigroeg, was known to many for her intelligence, and her sharp observational skills; she was also quite well known for her ability to "read" people, and for speaking her mind.

She was also the younger sister of Yikem Snave, that's why she was at the airport, saying goodbye to him.

Therefore, Yikem would tell her "Telepathically," with the use of pheromones what to say, and she could also tell Yikem, what she wanted to say, she also had permission to rephrase Yikem Snave's comments, if need be, because he could be a bit blunt at times.

Therefore, it was agreed, she would become the spokesperson on behalf of the F T W. Although Ycnan Snave or Haras Snave weren't too happy about the situation. However, they both had to concede that Eigroeg, was indeed the best ape for the job. So once again the meeting got underway, a request was put forward for humanity to be granted permission from the F T W, to restart the drilling for oil and gas, along with the right to restart coal mining, and to have all authority over the drilling and mining industries, promptly returned to them.

All of which Eigroeg Snave, with a simple shake of her head in a side to side no gesture, promptly rejected their proposal as completely unnecessary, because humanity had managed to survive without using any fossil fuel for a year. And to be honest, not having the use of fossil fuels was the least of their problems, as they were to discover very soon.

Because Eigroeg Snave, was about to put forward a proposition of her own, and as she told them, in her well-educated, softly spoken voice, what her proposals were, she could not believe the looks of disbelief, and utter astonishment, on the human faces.

One person actually looked under the table, to see if someone was hiding underneath, and doing the talking for her, another one (accidently,) blurted out how they could make an absolute fortune on her if they sold her to the highest bidder. Much to the dismay of Colonel Adams, who was seen holding his head in his hands in total disbelief at his colleagues' behavior.

And the official received a severe telling off from both Eigroeg and the Colonel, for doubting her ability to speak to humans, while the one that blurted the selling her comment, was instantly removed by his fellow representatives, and they physically threw him out of the fallout shelter.

And once they'd all returned to their seats, whilst apologizing profusely for insulting her, things settled down, and Eigroeg carried on with what she'd been saying.

Then after a very short pause to take in a breath. and just to put the icing on the cake, and to emphasise the comment, she told them she could also speak fluently in any language they chose. At which point Yikem burst out laughing, because these humans with their so-called "superior intelligence," that they so loved to brag about, could not believe that a dumb animal such as a mountain gorilla, could not only speak English, but was also more than capable of speaking fluently in any, and every language known to man.

And even though these people had received a formal and very precise briefing and had been told, long before the meeting took place how most, if not all, of these animals could talk verbally, not one of them truly believed it was possible. And the shock of it being true was now written all over their faces, especially the ones that had ridiculed Yikem and his associates, when they'd shared the helicopter with him and his colleagues. Yikem and his fellow Ambassadors, were now staring directly at them, and smiling a rather smug, you're not so clever now, are you? Smile at them.

Now, the proposition Eigroeg Snave put forward, was for humanity to promise never to dig or drill for fossil fuels ever again. She also demanded that all the oil and gas rigs, along with the coal, cadmium, lithium, gold, silver, and diamond mines, had to be destroyed, and permanently sealed.

In other words, if it was in the ground or the bottom of the ocean then it stays there. Mankind would now have no choice but to use renewable energy sources. They were also told how all the pollution, and needless destruction of the rainforests and its wildlife, would be stopped immediately. The same thing would apply to every living thing, both on land and in the sea. She then explained, that if humans carry on fishing at the same rate as they are now, then there would be no commercially viable fish left to catch in a maximum of forty years' time. (This is a true and proven fact.)

So, they would now have to create a renewable source, such as fish farming, they would also have to learn to respect what they have, instead of taking everything for granted, and being so wasteful, because their "throwaway society" no longer existed.

She then stated, how humanity must stop needlessly killing things for so-called "sport" or "trophy hunting," and to leave all the endangered animals (which included the Mountain gorillas) alone to recover.

Furthermore, if anyone was caught, or even suspected of poaching, then they would automatically be put to a very slow, and painful death, just like the poacher's victims, which would be carried out by the F T W, and the same thing would apply to anyone caught selling or buying ivory, tiger bones, rhino horn, or any type of animal skins or animal products such as bear gall bladder bile etc. In addition, every weapon in the world, would have to be destroyed within one month of this meeting.

By this she explained, meant all missiles, bombs, tanks, submarines, and guns, including all gun and or bomb-carrying planes and helicopters, would be destroyed worldwide.

And of course, this would also be done by the F T W who she (quite cheerily,) pointed out, already knew the exact number of each, and every weapon, and its whereabouts on the entire planet.

Of course, this was quickly rejected, and called a ridiculous proposal, some of the humans laughed quite loudly at the idea, (although to be honest, it appeared to be more of a nervous laugh, than one of ridicule.)

Then you could have heard a pin drop, when, just to prove her point, and to finally drive the message home, Eigroeg Snave looked the Colonel straight in the eye, and with a very serious tone to her well-educated softly spoken voice replied. You don't seem to understand what I am saying to you Colonel, so please listen carefully, and believe me when I tell you, that this is by no means a request, in fact, this is it, your last chance, so I suggest you think long and hard before you give me your answer.

Because, in case you haven't noticed, your species are no longer in charge of anything. And you're all slowly starving or freezing to death. You are also running a very serious risk of being killed by marauding gangs of vigilantes, so you really don't have any say whatsoever in the matter.

And you really do need to address the situation and come to terms with it, and the sooner the better. Because if you don't agree to meet, and honour our proposal, then we will just go ahead and destroy all your weapons anyway, as I've said we already know where and how many there are.

We have teams on standby at this very moment, at all the locations where the weapons are stored, just waiting for the order to go and destroy them all, regardless of whether you say yes or no. But, just out of common courtesy, we thought it only fair to ask your permission, mainly to see just how genuine you were about your offer to peacefully share this world with us, by that I mean every other living organism on the planet.

Now if you agree to these terms, then we will help you regain law and order over your own kind, and in any other way possible. So, we can all live peacefully side-by-side, with you in your world, and us in ours. If you respect us, then we will return that respect. However, if you decide to decline our offer, then we will quite simply sit back, and watch your species slowly starve yourselves to death, and into extinction, in the same way as the majority of your species have sat back and watched countless numbers of animals, insects, and plants, become extinct, simply because of your greed, and the fact you don't give a damn about the damage that your species have done, and are still doing to this planet, and have made no attempt whatsoever to stop it, in fact, you're still actively encouraging it.

So, the choice is yours, you have twenty-four hours to discuss your options, and to give us your answer. In the meantime, we will temporarily turn on your telecommunication systems, so you can talk with your superiors, although we will of course be monitoring your calls, just in case you foolishly decide to try anything.

Please remember one thing, and that is we are merely the mouthpiece of the F T W, and are expendable, so it would be pointless attempting to kidnap, or threaten us in any way. Also, if I may just add one more comment, which is, if you did try anything, then I can guarantee you one thing. Which is, there would be some major reprisals made on your species, oh, and not to put too fine a point on it, there is just one more thing for you to consider, which is, I can personally guarantee, that not a single one of you humans would leave this place alive.

At this point, Colonel Glyn Adams jumped to his feet, and started shouting for the guards to come in and arrest them. (The F T W had stated while the arrangements for the meeting were being made, that as a goodwill gesture, the F T W would not be bringing any of their security personnel into the meeting.)

The F T W just remained calmly in their seats, safe in the knowledge that no one would come, as the human guards had already been subdued by the F T W security, that had quietly entered the building twenty minutes after the meeting had started, and had quite easily overcome the guards, that had been quite happily sat in their canteen drinking tea, and playing cards, without a care in the world.

And when the humans in the meeting room finally realized that no one was coming to "save them", the humans did what most humans do in a crisis. They went into a blind panic, believing they were all going to be killed, and most probably eaten by these mountain gorillas. Except for Colonel Adams, who for most of the meeting had just been sat quietly studying every member of the F T W, and he'd concluded that Yikem Snave, although not actually saying anything, was in fact the one in charge. Because although he appeared to be quite nonchalant, and disinterested in the whole thing, the Colonel also had a feeling that Yikem Snave was somehow telling Eigroeg Snave what to say.

Now, being a shrewd man, and based on his observations, along with the way they interacted with each other, he also concluded that the two of them are most certainly related. And not just by name.

So, while every member of his team was running around screaming like little girls who had just found a big hairy spider in the bed, the F

T W were just sat there laughing inwardly to themselves, at just how pathetically feeble, and defenceless these humans really were, without their technological backup.

Colonel Adams slowly raised himself out of his chair, walked forwards, and approached Yikem Snave, who was watching the Colonel intently as he did so, and so were Yikem's associates, (who had already been told to stay where they were.)

The Colonel, smiled at Yikem as he approached him, and was holding out his hand as a token of friendship, he then said, nicely done, you appear to be a lot more intelligent than we originally thought.

And most certainly, a lot more organised than the rabble I've been lumbered with, waving his hand towards his panic-stricken colleagues, but never taking his eyes off Yikem.

The Colonel once more held his hand out, and once more, it remained ignored and unshaken. Then with a smile, the Colonel asked if there was any chance of just the two of them having a word in private.

To which Eigroeg Snave sharply replied, you would have to speak to him through me, as Yikem Snave doesn't talk. To which Colonel Adams, who once more, never taking his eyes of Yikem, simply smiled, and replied, please, don't place me in the same category as these hopeless morons. And once again, without taking his eyes off Yikem, waved his hand towards his associates, who were still running around screaming.

I know Yikem Snave is the person in charge. And I also know you're just the mouthpiece, saying what you're told, which of course made Eigroeg Snave very angry.

And as she stood up to respond to the comment made, Yikem held his hand up, and Eigroeg stopped dead in her tracks. (Much to Yikem's surprise.) Yikem, then spoke for the first time, stating that the Colonel was indeed a very astute and shrewd man. He also mentioned how the Colonel appeared to be somewhat "different," to the other humans, and how both Yikem and the Colonel just "clicked," and seemed to have a mutual, and instinctive respect for each other.

So, they agreed to go into a separate and more peaceful room to talk things through, much to the dismay of Eigroeg and associates. But then Yikem Snave reassured them that they would hear every word spoken, and if he felt threatened in any way, he would let them know.

At which point Colonel Adams added, Yikem is at least five times stronger than I am, plus I have just personally witnessed him shake and then throw a fully-grown man as if he were nothing more than a rag doll. Therefore, I know just how strong he is, so if anyone should be feeling threatened then I think I have a lot more to worry about than your associate.

And so, it was settled, The Colonel and Yikem Snave went off to try to find some "common ground" on which they could build, and they both hoped it would lead to some sort of agreement being made. Or at the very least, some sort of compromise, that they would both be willing to pursue.

Now during the next three hours, (that passed surprisingly quickly,) while they put their case to each other, and discussed their options. Colonel Adams panic-stricken associates had finally calmed down. And had now realised they were not going to be killed, or eaten, by the remaining F T W ambassadors after all.

So, they were all now sat rather sheepishly in their seats, directly opposite the F T W, who were all staring intently at them as they squirmed and twitched nervously, trying their best to hide their embarrassment of what had just happened, which of course, just added to the amusement of the F T W.

So Eigroeg Snave, (with good intention) tried her best to make a joke of what had happened, in an attempt to break the ice, by mentioning to Colonel Adams colleagues, just how lucky they were that none of the F T W was hungry, because they had all eaten, just before they'd left for the meeting.

Now, this really didn't help matters in the slightest, because the humans already overactive imagination had now started to run amok, conjuring visions of people being ripped apart, limb from limb, whilst still alive, and then being eaten. Plus, they could still feel the evil eye they were getting off the F T W. that was sat less than two metres away burning into them. This resulted in the humans laughing and giggling hysterically, in a feeble attempt to hide their nervousness.

And they were now beginning to get extremely "twitchy," to say the least, and a few of them were quite visibly shaking, and sweating with fear, plus the numerous visits to the lavatory, really didn't help them in the slightest, because to get to the lavatories they had to walk within a metre and a half of the F T W.

Much to the delight of the now seriously bored ambassadors, who had slowly and rather sneakily been moving their seats closer and closer towards the toilet door, which was now only a metre away, and they were thoroughly enjoying themselves by toying with them.

Each person that passed them, was greeted with a low guttural growl, accompanied of course, by the "evil eye" glare as they approached.

Some of the human representatives also received a feigned attack, as one of the F T W ambassadors whose name was Ytnom Ytnom, who just for the sheer devilment of it would suddenly lurch forward, as if attacking, but would then suddenly stop, whilst giving the poor human on the receiving end, such an evil stare that the man then really did need to use the toilet, and quickly.

Which of course, the other Ambassadors, (and Eigroeg) found highly amusing, however, the F T W was now starting to get a little bit too boisterous. Although there was no actual malice intended in their actions, they really didn't mean any harm, as they were only toying with them out of boredom, just like a group of teasing, and mischievous children.

However, Eigroeg Snave, who had been thoroughly enjoying the show, now unfortunately, had no option but to tell the human representatives that she had been joking when she made the not hungry comment, because Mountain Gorillas were, in fact, vegetarians.

Much to the disappointment of her friends, who had been quite happily sat watching them sweat and squirm. Eventually, one of the humans attempted to break the silence, by trying in vain to start a conversation with Eigroeg, by asking her if she had been educated in the United Kingdom.

And if so, what was the name of the university she had attended to learn to speak English so perfectly? Along with the many other languages, she was apparently so impeccably fluent in, which resulted in every member of the F T W falling about in fits of laughter, for asking such a stupid question. Except for Eigroeg, who just sat there staring at him, in disbelief, with a dumbfounded look on her face, whilst thinking to herself, did you really just ask where I learned to speak English?

And the person who made the comment realised what he had said and tried to apologize, by saying oh dear, I do apologize most profusely madam, I didn't mean to appear to be prying into your private life, I was just curious, which just made things worse.

So, one of his associates, wisely told him (very abruptly,) and rather loudly, to shut his big mouth, before someone fell in it, and every time the person who made the comment went to use the toilet, the F T W couldn't even manage to growl at him, simply because they were too busy laughing as they kept repeating "telepathically," to themselves, madam? Madam?

Which just made them laugh even louder, until eventually; they couldn't even look at him without falling about laughing, and now, because they'd laughed so much, it was starting to hurt. Which really confused the human representative, because he could not, for the life of him, work out what was so funny? So, after five hours of discussion, Colonel Adams and Yikem Snave agreed to stop for the day, with both agreeing to talk to their superiors.

And hopefully, just the two of them could continue the discussion the next day. At which point they shook hands, thanked each other for their time, and for respecting each other's point of view, and commitment, to resolving the matter, so the meeting was called to an end, and they went their separate ways.

A few minutes later Colonel Adams could be heard quite plainly bellowing at his colleagues for letting the side down, and for embarrassing him in front of their guests, at which point the Colonel left them to it.

As the Colonel walked down the long passageway towards his quarters, he heard some muffled sounds, so he went to find out where these sounds were coming from, and what was causing them.

And that's when he accidentally stumbled across his "hand-picked" (but not by him) security staff, all of which were bound up tightly with industrial insulation tape, and cable ties, and then bundled into a storeroom. The air then turned blue, as he told every one of them exactly what he thought of them, he also told them if anything like this ever happened again, then he would personally, put every single one of them, one, by one, against a wall, and shoot them.

Now, the men had heard enough stories about the Colonel, to know he meant every word he had said. And then the Colonel left them, still tied up in the storeroom, where he had found them.

As he walked away, he could be heard (very loudly,) ordering them to be in his office in full parade uniform, in exactly one hour, and anyone failing to attend would be court marshalled, and drummed out of their regiment in disgrace.

Yikem and co could be heard laughing raucously, as the soulful moan let out by the disheartened guards, who knew full well, that none of them would make it to the Colonels office in time, reached their ears.

At one-point Yikem briefly considered untying them, as a token of goodwill, but then decide against it, and thought how he would love to be a fly on the wall in that office in one hours' time. Which of course he personally couldn't do, and then the very slightest of smirks played ever so briefly across his face, as he realized he knew a fly that could.

Then it dawned on him, that his colleagues had "picked up" on his thoughts and were giving him a "surely you are joking right," sort of look. So, he looked back at them with feigned innocence, put both his arms in the air and said Well why not?

And how it would be for intelligence purposes only, knowing full well, that it would be monitored anyway, although the humans, had no idea whatsoever that this was the case, at which point they all shook their heads in disbelief, and walked away, leaving just Yikem and Eigroeg alone, staring at each other, and Yikem still acting the fool, pretending to be all innocent, saying what? what? To her, with a mischievous smile all over his face.

But just like any sister, all she could do was smile back at him with a, you really are something else, look on her face, then she just reached out and ruffled the hair on his head as if he were nothing more than a mischievous little schoolboy, rather than the main representative of every single animal and insect on this planet.

Yet, she had to admit to herself, that it was nice to end the day on a happy note. So, after a long, and somewhat restless night, because Yikem was being constantly bombarded with questions, along with quite a few suggestions, from all over the world, until at 0.300 hours, he had no choice but to "shut down" so no one could contact him.

Eventually, daybreak finally arrived, and at 0.700 hours precisely, his aide knocked on Yikem's door, and once told to enter, asked Yikem if he slept well, and would he be requiring breakfast? To which Yikem replied (rather abruptly,) no, to both questions, his aide, then reminded Yikem of his appointment with Colonel Adams at 0.900 hours, to which Yikem snapped, I know that, back at him, so the aide just politely nodded in agreement, then quickly left, and the aide was now somewhat concerned about Yikem's temperament and went to speak to Eigroeg about it.

Although she reassured him that everything would be fine, and how she would speak to Yikem before his meeting with the Colonel, the aide remained somewhat uneasy.

Eventually Eigroeg convinced him that everything would be fine, and off he went about his business. Now, as soon as the previous meeting had ended, all telecommunications were, as promised, reconnected, and Colonel Adams was made aware of this, so he spent the entire night talking to his superiors, but not before making an official complaint against all the human representatives, who had made a complete mockery of both the meeting, and themselves.

Along with the "hand-picked" guard's lackluster behaviour, and true to his word he put in a request to have them all court-martialed for dereliction of duty, (as none of them made it to the Colonels office in the one-hour deadline.) The Colonel, then explained in detail, what had been said at the meeting. He also told them all about Yikem Snave's behaviour, he also mentioned that Yikem Snave was the "main man" in this conference, and he was certain Eigroeg Snave was second in command, and he believed they were somehow related to each other.

He then told them how he would find a way to send a message to his superiors; outlining possible ways to use this bond against them somehow if the need arose.

The Colonel also explained how the F T W was monitoring every phone call, so he had to be very careful what he said. Obviously, he never actually said those words, instead he used certain words in his conversation that had specific meanings and were part of a pre-planned code, and once that was done, he told his superiors, (this time in plain English) that he didn't think there would be any agreements reached during this meeting. But how he was hopeful of creating some common ground, with Yikem Snave, to which his superior, angrily ordered the Colonel to "get it sorted," and to get an agreement handing everything back to us signed, as soon as possible, preferably by the end of the day. And how he shouldn't take any more shit from these jumped-up monkeys.

So, the Colonel sarcastically, invited his superior to leave his comfortable office in London, and to come and tell these "monkeys," in person, and promptly hung up on him. Then, just as he was leaving his office the phone started ringing, but he knew who it was, and decided to ignore it, and as he opened his office door, his aide, who was just about to enter the room, heard him muttering, arsehole, and how it was going to be one of those days to himself.

Now Yikem's aide had also overheard his comment, and thought to himself, you really don't know the half of it, and immediately set off in search of Eigroeg, as he once again had a bad feeling about the consequences of the meeting that was due to start in the next thirty minutes.

Once again, Eigroeg reassured him everything would be okay, so when he finally calmed down, he asked if there was anything he could do to help.

To which she replied, no, not now thank you Igoy, but if I do, be assured I will let you know. Which seemed to make him a bit more relaxed, and off he went to see if Yikem required anything. Now, fifteen minutes before the meeting was due to start, Ycnan Snave had contacted both Yikem and Eigroeg, and they were told that Eigroeg had to attend the meeting alongside Yikem, in order to keep the peace, and that the decision, wasn't open for discussion.

So, they both went into the meeting room five minutes early, to find Colonel Adams already sat at the table, with a telephone on one side of him, and a large mug of coffee on the other, along with a small mountain of paperwork, directly in front of him.

The Colonel, stood up, and greeted them both as if they were old friends, (which immediately put both Yikem and Eigroeg on their guard,) and once everyone had said good morning to each other, the Colonel said he was glad that Eigroeg was also involved. And how he hoped that between the three of them, they could come to a mutually beneficial agreement, but what he was really thinking was great, now I can keep an eye on the two of you.

So, after another brief exchange of pleasantries such as, I hope everything in your quarters is to your satisfaction. Along with the usual, did you sleep okay? (Knowing full well that no one had any sleep) they decided to get on with the meeting, Colonel Adams started the conversation with these words. My superiors did not take too kindly to the threats that were made on behalf of your organization.

Especially, the fact that you stated how you intended to sit back, and watch humanity slowly starve to death. They are also somewhat peeved about your threats to destroy all our weapons. And I have been given strict orders from my superiors to get this problem resolved today.

I have also been instructed, by the prime minister himself to, and I quote, don't take any more shit off these jumped-up monkeys, and how he wants an agreement signed by the F T W today, thereby handing everything back to us. At which point I invited him to come here and tell these "monkeys" himself, but for some reason, he declined my offer.

Obviously, Yikem and Eigroeg didn't take to kindly to being called monkeys. Yikem was now on his feet, and rapidly heading towards the Colonel, (who was stood there ready for the fight) and was just about to grab the man by the throat, however, as Eigroeg was quick to point out, that you had to respect the Colonel for his honesty. And that comment literally saved the Colonels life, because Yikem was not in the best of moods as it was, and neither was the Colonel, so the Colonel tried the diplomatic approach, and was busily highlighting how humanity, would now be willing to reconsider their position as the superior beings. And how they would now be more than willing to abandon the use of fossil fuels in favour of renewable energy, however, they would need access to their fossil fuel reserves, to produce the solar panels, along with the wind and water turbines. All of which was promptly rejected as unnecessary by both Yikem and Eigroeg because mankind was already producing these things without the use of fossil fuels, and had been doing so for just over a year, then Yikem commented, look Colonel, please don't insult our intelligence again? To which the Colonel replied, you're not going to make this easy for me are you? In an attempt to lighten the mood, but he received no reply as his answer.

So once again, Eigroeg repeated her proposal, and once again, the Colonel rejected it, because there was no way the "powers that be" would accept such a proposal, on the grounds that they would be vulnerable to attack from other countries. Therefore, it was again pointed out to the Colonel, how mankind, no longer had any" powers that be." And that it would be a worldwide destruction of weapons, and not just the United Kingdom, as he seemed to think.

So, Colonel Adams asked if it would be possible for him to ring the Prime minister, to explain the offer to him in greater detail. And Yikem replied, whilst pointing at the phone, please, feel free, then Eigroeg said in a rather stern voice, I would also like to have a word with him.

Colonel Adams just smiled and said I'll see what I can do, whilst thinking to himself, oh don't you worry, I'm banking on it. Then the Colonel said, (tongue in cheek) if it is possible for you to talk to the prime minister, please remember one thing, and that is he is the man in charge of this country, so please treat him with the respect he deserves. To which Eigroeg replied, he has no authority whatsoever over me, or any other member of our organization, however, as long as he listens and respects what I have to say, then I will do the same for him. So, the Colonel made the call, but unbeknown to Yikem, or Eigroeg, just as the prime minister answered the phone, the Colonel, knowing full well that the prime minister would make some sort of smart-arse remark "accidentally" (and rather sneakily) turned on the speakerphone.

And before anyone could say anything, everyone heard the prime minister saying (rather sarcastically) to the Colonel, well. Have you got those stupid monkeys to sign everything back over to us then?

And the Colonel replied in a rather shocked voice (as if he had no idea how the speaker was turned on) um no, no, not yet sir, he then told the prime minister, I really must apologize. But somehow the phone was on the loudspeaker setting, and the members of the F T W that are sitting at the table with me now, have also heard your monkey comment, and by the look on their faces, they don't appear to be overly impressed by what you just said, sir. And with the loudspeaker still turned on, the prime minister replied, well you can tell them from me (but mid-sentence) the Colonel had handed the phone to Eigroeg, (although the handset wasn't needed,) it was more of a there you go then, your turn, gesture. Now Eigroeg, much to the Colonels surprise, had just sat there quietly with Yikem, and there was no visible trace of anger (or come to that any other emotion,) on their faces.

However, as I said Eigroeg now had the phone, and the Colonel was sitting there expectantly waiting for her to start hurling abuse at the country's leader.

But, once again, she just sat there quietly, listening to the prime minister making all sorts of ludicrous threats, such as you tell them monkeys if they don't sign things back to us immediately, then we will bomb their jungle home, we'll kill the lot of them, and I'll hang their heads on my drawing room wall. And he carried on ranting and raving for at least ten more minutes, then he went quiet for a few seconds, then suddenly he screamed down the phone, are you listening to me Adams?

But, instead of the Colonels deep voice, he heard a quiet and well-educated female voice reply, oh yes prime minister, I'm listening intently to every word, and the prime minister replied, who the hell are you, the secretary?

So Eigroeg (quite calmly) introduced herself, she then heard the prime minister say quietly under his breath, oh shit, and Eigroeg replied to his comment with, well, if you've quite finished, I would also like to say something to you.

And that is, the F T W were more than willing to help you regain control of your species, we were also, more than willing to consider any sensible compromises you may have put forward, however, after listening to your insane ranting for the last ten minutes or so, insulting and threatening to bomb our home, and killing my family, which by the way would be an impossible thing for you to do, because none of your aircraft are capable of taking off without our permission. And secondly, you will never have access to any of your bombs or come to that any other weapon to use against us. Therefore, I think that now puts you, along with the remainder of your species in a very unfavourable position at the moment, so I strongly advise you to apologize for the threats you've made. And you really need to listen very carefully to what I have to say to you.

First of all, if you make any attempt whatsoever, to follow through with any of the threats you've just made, then I can personally guarantee it will be the last thing you'll ever do in this life. Secondly, I strongly advise you to listen very carefully to what Colonel Adams has to say, and just as she finished the last sentence, the prime minister replied, (in a very angry tone) you don't tell me what I can or can't do, you do know who you're talking to do you? Then he demanded to speak to the Colonel, he also demanded they turned the speaker off.

However, Eigroeg had by no means finished talking, oh no, not by a long way, so she ignored his demands and carried on quite calmly with what she had to say, and the Colonel just couldn't believe how calm and collected both Eigroeg and Yikem were. So Eigroeg said to the prime minister, right, if you've quite finished ranting, this is the way things are going to be done from now on.

The F T W will never, under any circumstances return authority back to you humans, quiet simply because you just abuse it, so you can forget that one for a start. You can also stop putting poisons down in our jungle home in your feeble attempts to kill us, because we have collected all the poisons and they are now in the United Kingdom's main water supply. So, if you were wondering why so many people have suddenly died in the last few days, then now you have the answer.

And you can take my word for it, it wouldn't be that difficult to put some of it into your personal water supply at number ten Downing Street, then you'd know first-hand what it's like to watch your children die a slow, and very painful death. Oh, and by the way, before you reply to my last statement, let me just tell you that every single word you have said so far, has also been heard by every single animal and insect on this planet.

The prime minister responded to these remarks, (especially the one about poisoning his water supply,) with another torrent of abuse about how you stupid monkeys can't tell me what I can and can't do. And how they would never be able to get into number 10, because the security had been substantially increased, and how the F T W had just made a very big mistake by threatening to kill his children.

So, Eigroeg replied with, oh! okay then, so it's all right for you to kill my family with poison. But we can't do the same to you humans; well as far as I'm concerned Mr. prime minister, you have just proven that you are nothing more than a loud-mouthed hypocrite and have absolutely no intention whatsoever of trying to find a way in which we could all live together peacefully.

Plus, if you'd been listening to what I said, you would have realized that I never actually threatened you, or your family, as all I said was it wouldn't be that difficult to do so, if we were that way inclined.

And then like a fool, the prime minister replied, well you're more than welcome to try, but I can tell you now you won't get within one hundred yards of number ten. To which Eigroeg replied oh, okay then, I'll expect another call from you within the hour. And hung up on him.

Which left the prime minister somewhat confused, and very angry and frustrated, and he was now stomping around number ten like a spoilt child that couldn't get its own way, and shouting at the top of his voice, I hate smart arse monkeys that try to tell me what to do. The damn cheek of it.

The Colonel, who had heard everything that was said by both parties, asked Eigroeg. what was the... I'll expect your phone call within the hour all about. Eigroeg replied he's just set me a challenge, and I fully intend to complete it, Yikem was now a little worried that she was intending to poison the prime minister and his family, so she explained "telepathically" that she had no intention of doing any such thing. (As tempting as it may be.)

So, she had now managed to confuse both her brother and the Colonel, who were both just sat there staring at each other, with a what the hell was that all about look on their faces. (Which briefly made Eigroeg smile) so the Colonel (halfheartedly) started to apologize to them on behalf of the prime minister, and while he was doing so Eigroeg was busy organizing a little surprise for the country's leader, but now, Yikem was in on it as well. And it was all he could do to keep a straight face as the Colonel carried on talking away, pretty much to himself, because Yikem was barely listening to what he was saying and occasionally nodded his head (hopefully in the right places) as if in agreement with the Colonel. And Eigroeg most certainly wasn't listening, because she was just putting the finishing touches to the prime minister's little surprise.

In the meantime, the Colonel carried on waffling away to himself for another three-quarters of an hour or so, then thankfully, (because both Yikem and Eigroeg were now in serious danger of nodding off,) the phone started ringing, but this time, both Eigroeg and Yikem said simultaneously keep it on speaker if you don't mind, please Colonel. To which he replied (with a somewhat confused look still on his face) certainly, and Yikem and Eigroeg just nodded and smiled.

And sure, enough it was the prime minister, however, this time, he had a very different, slightly worried, tone to his voice, and he immediately asked to speak to the female again, which didn't go down to well with either Eigroeg or Yikem.

(Come to that, Colonel Adams didn't appear to be overly impressed either) because the man so obviously couldn't even be bothered to remember Eigroeg's name, and they now also doubted whether he had any idea that he was talking to a Mountain Gorilla, even though Eigroeg had formally introduced herself to him during the first phone call.

However, all the prime minister (somewhat sheepishly) had to say was, okay, you've proven your point. Now could you please remove the ants that had descended on number ten in their millions (and not one of the many security officers spotted a single one of them) as they climbed up the exterior wall, under the roof tiles and roofing felt, then down through the loft (following the electrical cables) into the ceiling lights and chewing their way through the plastic ceiling roses, then along the ceiling, down the walls and the staircase and eventually just casually strolling into where the prime minister and his family were sat quietly watching a film on their DVD player.

(Obviously, they couldn't get any channels on their television because everything had been shut down for the past twelve months) and they didn't see, or hear anything, until the fire ants started biting them, just enough for them to know they were there. Now fire ants get their name simply because when they bite you it feels as if the area that's been bitten is on fire, and it's a very painful bite.

The fire ants also attacked and destroyed all the electrical goods on the premises, including the household's main incoming electrical supply, which also included the backup generator they had in number ten, because as I mentioned earlier, fire ants are unexplainably attracted to any machinery that gives off a high electrical pulse.

And in some countries, they cost air traffic control millions of pounds a year in repair bills, because they like to eat through the power cables. (True fact) and then, as suddenly as they'd appeared, the fire ants vanished, only staying long enough to prove a point.

However, they were still in the house, just in case they needed to prove that point once more, plus they were now in a position to listen in on any plans of attack being made.

However, the prime minister at the moment was more concerned about another and more important matter. Because two of his children who are aged ten and twelve years old, had to go to hospital because they were in so much pain, although most of it was shock of being "attacked" in their own home, all of which he explained in great detail to a very uninterested Eigroeg, who just (very coldly) replied, well believe me, it could have been a lot worse. It could quite easily have been poison in your water tank, and you should be thankful that we're not as hard-hearted, self-centred or as callous as you humans, because we have no intention of hurting or killing anyone, or anything.

But please don't think for one minute that this is a sign of weakness on our part, because believe me, it doesn't mean we won't do so if we must.

So, the prime minister realized (in a rather unsavoury way) as the Colonel had, that he had grossly underestimated the intelligence and organizational skills of the F T W, and while the prime minister was still pouring his heart out about his children being in so much pain, and how she had absolutely no right whatsoever, to sanction such a cruel and very personal attack against him and his family to her.

At which point Eigroeg, who was now bored with listening to the Prime ministers constant pathetic whining, had handed the phone back to the Colonel. Although once again the handset wasn't really needed because the speaker was still on, and was merely done as a symbolic gesture, and she told the Colonel, can you please speak to this moron! As I have no time for arrogant, self-righteous, sanctimonious hypocrites, who think it's okay to torture animals in laboratories, or to catch them in snares for their fur, or bones. But, when the tables are turned on them, they become gutless whining imbeciles, just like your so-called leader.

(All of which the prime minister heard,) and with that Eigroeg, and Yikem stood up, and headed for the door, and as they were leaving, Yikem turned around and said to Colonel Adams, you really need to sort that twat out mate.

You know where we are when you want to talk, however, I don't expect that will happen until tomorrow, (although it was only just coming up to dinner time now,) as I expect you have a lot to talk about with your "friend," just don't take any shit off the man. He may be above you, but he most certainly isn't better than you, if you know what I mean.

To which Eigroeg replied "telepathically," ooh, so you've made a friend there, you'll be looking at curtains and soft furnishings with him next. Which Yikem thought was a bit on the harsh side, especially for her, and there wasn't even the slightest sign of any humour either in her words or on her face, so once they had left the Colonels office Yikem asked Eigroeg what was wrong with her? And she replied, (rather snappily,) don't be a fool Yikem, you don't honestly think for one minute that that man is your friend, do you? Because the man is a professional soldier, he's been trained to make people feel comfortable and relaxed in his presence, simply because if someone classes you as a friend and trusts you, then they are much easier to manipulate.

So be warned, because I have watched the two of you and you seem to have "clicked" with each other. Now I hope I'm wrong, but all I can say is please, don't ever think for one minute that the two of you could ever be friends or allies in this war. Because that's what this is Yikem, it's not a game we're playing here, and make no mistake it will get a whole lot worse before it ever gets any better, and let's leave it at that for now then, shall we.

She then walked away, and left Yikem wondering once more, what the hell was that all about? She had also "shut down" so no one could know what she was thinking. (I don't really think she knew herself to be honest,) and no one could get in touch with her, not even Ycnan Snave, who of course had "heard" the whole conversation, so, Ycnan decided to leave it for a while. Because it wouldn't be any good trying to talk to Yikem, as his thoughts were also a bit on the erratic side, to say the least at the moment, plus Ycnan was a bit on the busy side herself, as she was personally monitoring the ongoing conversation between Colonel Adams and the prime minister. Which at the moment really wasn't going in the prime ministers' favour, (and hadn't been for the last hour or so) because Colonel Adams had taken Yikem's advice, and he was really ripping into the prime minister about how he had handled his conversation with Eigroeg, and not even bothering to remember her name.

Or even acknowledging the fact that he knew he was talking to a Mountain Gorilla, who was also one of the main ambassadors for the F T W, to which the prime minister replied, well to be honest with you Glyn, I didn't know that I was talking to a gorilla.

Colonel Adams then replied (very sternly) don't you ever, have the audacity to call me by my first name again, only my family and close friends call me Glyn, and you are most definitely not on that list, and I doubt very much if you ever would be.

So once again the prime minister got on his high horse and started making ridiculous demands on the Colonel as to how he should handle the present situation, so the Colonel told him quite firmly, (using a slightly more colourful phrase than I've used here) to shut his mouth, and to come and deal with the F T W himself.

Because he seemed to have all the answers, however, it would be a very different situation when he had to talk face to face with them, all sat in the same room, and less than two metres away from you, rather than hundreds of miles away in relative safety. However, the Colonel (quite cheerily) was quick to point out to the prime minister that they had already proven, without a doubt, that if they wanted to get at him or his family they could very easily do so. And before the prime minister could say anything the Colonel said now piss off you twat, and hung up on him, before the prime minister had a chance to reply.

The Colonel, who was now physically shaking with temper and frustration, because the only thing the prime minister appeared to be interested in now, was revenge on the F T W for daring to attack him and his family. Therefore, the Colonel went in search of either Yikem, or Eigroeg, to ask them to turn all communication systems off again, because they were more trouble than help.

And if anybody had any more bright ideas on how he should sort this mess out, then they could come and tell the F T W themselves, because he'd really had enough of people telling him what to do from the safety of being hundreds of miles away. Sat in a nice warm office without the slightest idea, and therefore no way involved in what was going on. Eigroeg was the first one he found, and she promptly done as he asked, and all communication with the outside world were once more disconnected.

 She now also realized just how pissed off the Colonel was, especially when he turned and said to her, (looking her straight in the eye,) maybe I'm on the wrong side in this battle, perhaps, I should join forces with your lot? At least you know what you're doing, and more importantly, you also appear to know how to do it.

And while he was saying this, he was studying Eigroeg's face intently, looking for even the slightest sign of acceptance, but he saw nothing, not even in her eyes not so much as a flicker, and I dare say, if he had seen even the slightest of glimmers, he would have joined the F T W there and then.

However, he saw absolutely nothing at all, so the Colonel thanked Eigroeg for turning the communications off, then turning sharply on his heel, he walked away, before Eigroeg had a chance to say your welcome, which, with hindsight, was just as well. Because it could quite easily have been taken by the Colonel, in his confused state of mind, as an invitation to join the F T W, and not as a polite remark made in acknowledgment of his thank you for turning the communications off.

Now, all of this had happened from just before dinnertime, up until now, which was teatime. Which may sound a rather odd way of telling the time, but to a mountain gorilla, it's ideal. Because they normally spend a great deal of their time either eating, looking for food, or sleeping, although I wouldn't advise any human to say that to one of them in person, (unless of course that person just happened to be the prime minister of this country.)

Therefore, the day's talks had come to a sudden, and grinding halt at five pm, (teatime) and you could have cut the atmosphere in the place with a knife.

No one saw hide nor hair of the Colonel, Eigroeg, or Yikem for the rest of the evening, as strict orders were given stating that under no circumstances, were they to be disturbed. And nobody knows to this day, what they were doing that evening, because Eigroeg and Yikem had "shutdown," and the Colonel never left his quarters. Maybe they decided to catch up on some much-needed rest? However, as I've already said, we will never know the answer to that one, but various ideas have been put forward.

Anyway, once again, morning arrives, and as usual Yikem's aide arrives at 0.700 hours precisely, (breakfast time), knocked on Yikem's door, and once told to enter, the aide done so, and all he said to Yikem was is there anything I can do for you? Remembering how Yikem had snapped at him the last time the aide asked if he would be requiring breakfast that morning and reminding Yikem of his meeting with the Colonel. So, he decided to say as little as possible this morning, and surprisingly Yikem seemed to be in a very good mood indeed, and the first thing he said to his aide was, good morning Igoy, which was quickly followed by, what delights have we got for breakfast today then?

This caught the aide completely off guard, because Yikem very rarely called any of his staff by their first names, but not because he classed himself as above them, it's simply because he has always been useless at remembering names. So, the aide told Yikem what the choices were, and Yikem replied with a smile, I tell you what Igoy, why don't you surprise me, and you make the choice for me? To which the aide replied, (in a somewhat confused voice,) as you wish sir, and promptly left the room, (slightly faster than he normally would,) because he couldn't understand how Yikem was so full of the joys of life, especially after what had happened the previous day.

And when the aide Igoy returned with a trolley full to the brim with food, it was Yikem's turn to look somewhat confused, until the aide, (seeing the confused look on Yikem's face,) said I wasn't sure what you would want. So, I brought it all, and Yikem fell about laughing, and when he'd finally finished, he stood up and slapped the aide heartily on the back, and said, Igoy my friend, you really are a good ape, and proceeded to choose what he wanted for breakfast. At which point Igoy, (again in a slightly confused voice,) replied, well thankyou sir, and quickly left the room.

Now the reason Yikem was so happy was because once he had "turned back on" he instantly received a message from Ycnan Snave. Saying how the British prime minister had made a statement that was "broadcasted" all around London, and every other major city in Britain by the local town crier, that the British government had decided to cease all hostile activity against the F T W. And how there would now be a concentrated effort made by the British government to start peace talks with them, in an attempt to try and find a way in which both parties would mutually benefit.

So, with a hearty breakfast inside him, Yikem was ready to start his day, and off he went in search of Colonel Adams to tell him the good news.

However, Eigroeg was already with the Colonel, and they were both sat calmly in the Colonels office discussing the ins and outs of the prime minister's statement, as Yikem entered the room, still full of the joys of life, but that was about to change, because he couldn't help but notice the rather serious look on both their faces. So, Yikem asked what's wrong? And hadn't they heard the good news?

Colonel Adams replied yes, your sister has told me all about it, and a rather stunned Yikem "telepathically" asked Eigroeg how the Colonel new she was his sister? And much to his surprise, Eigroeg replied verbally, because I told him, at this point Yikem exploded into a fit of rage and started shouting at his sister about how she herself had told him not to trust the Colonel, and how they could never be friends or allies in this war. Along with the fact they were told before they left their home to attend this meeting, that under no circumstances were they to give out any information about the F T W, let alone tell anyone that they were related.

And then the Colonel tried to intervene by saying to Yikem, you really need to sit down, and listen to what I have to say about the governments statement, so after a few minutes, along with a little helpful encouragement from Eigroeg, Yikem eventually calmed down enough to listen to what they both had to say.

The Colonel started by telling Yikem, that the statement wasn't what it appeared to be, and went on to explain that a lot of the statement was in fact, a coded message, which was intended for the Colonel. And the reason they released this statement is, because although all communication with the outside world have been disconnected, which I personally asked your sister to do, but your sister had also inadvertently told the prime minister, that every animal and insect on the planet was listening to the conversation she was having with him at the time.

Now, the prime minister, despite what many people may think, is by no means a fool, and he's obviously worked out that when this statement was released it would immediately be sent to you, knowing full well that one of you would also tell me about the good news. Because as I said, the message is intended for me.

Now, the cease all hostile activity is part of a coded message, which means, if I can't get a signed agreement from you by midnight tonight. Then I must end the meeting at 0.900 hours the following morning, with the instructions for you to go back and speak to your superiors. And the attempt at peace talks, means that I put you and your ambassadors on a separate helicopter to the human representatives, quite simply because the government now fully intend to blast you, and your colleagues, out of the air.

And the British Government would then pass it off as an unfortunate accident caused by faulty machinery, which they would then say was due to lack of maintenance, caused by not being able to access the necessary equipment needed to do the job, because of F T W restrictions, thereby placing the blame firmly on your organization.

So, a very shocked, and surprised Yikem replied, would you like us to turn the telecommunications back on, so you can speak to the prime minister? To which the Colonel replied. No not really, not at the moment thank you. Because I know I'll say something I'd regret later, so we'll leave it for now if you don't mind.

So Eigroeg and Yikem said, then if you'll excuse us for a moment, we need to sort this out one way or another, and surprisingly the Colonel replied if there's anything I can do to help you in any way then please don't hesitate to ask. And I give you my word that whatever we discuss will remain between us, and no one else needs to know.

Eigroeg said thank you to the Colonel, she and Yikem then left him in his office to ponder over what the F T W would do next, in the meantime Eigroeg had contacted Ycnan Snave and was discussing their options.

However, the one thing no one could understand was how the British government had managed to put together this coded message plan without the F T W picking up on it. This was worrying Ycnan Snave gravely, so she instructed Yikem and Eigroeg to try to discover where this coded message plan was discussed. Then Ycnan Snave told them that she had already given the order to destroy all the weapons several hours before the government statement was issued.

The destruction was due to start at 0.600 hrs. the following day so in theory they wouldn't have any weapons to use on the helicopter. Plus, most of the fuel, which had been reserved for the planes, tanks, etc., had been removed.

However, the F T W did leave a few thousand litres of fuel in every army, naval, and air force base throughout the country, for the sole purpose of getting the military staff to do the job for them, because the F T W had contaminated the fuel with finely crushed glass so when they tried to use it, it would destroy the engines.

And then Ycnan Snave asked them both if they thought the Colonels offer to help was a genuine one, or was he just trying to find out what the F T W intended to do about the threat? She also asked about the human researchers that offered to work undercover for them. And did they think they could be trusted because we need to get all of you out of that place as soon as we possibly can.

So, if you go back to the Colonel and tell him how the order to destroy all weapons had already been issued, and see what his response is; also, to check if the researchers offer was genuine. And once the major weapons and weapon carriers have been destroyed, I'll get in touch and let you know exactly what we intend to do.

But. I will tell you this, the F T W now intend to shut down all the remaining resources the humans have. including the hospitals all over the world. Because the F T W, as a sign of compassion, had left them all untouched and they were the only buildings that still had the water, gas, and electricity supplies still connected and were therefore heavily guarded by the military to stop any vigilante gangs from entering and stealing the much-needed drugs and medicines.

Now although the hospitals have emergency backup generators that will run for a minimum of forty-eight hours the F T W gave them an additional forty-eight hours' notice of their intention to disconnect them. Thereby giving them time to install solar panels and/or wind turbines, along with hydrogen cells, which would not only produce the electricity they needed, but it also produces drinking water in the process.

NASA use hydrogen cells to provide power and water on the space shuttles, (true fact.) So, Yikem and Eigroeg went and told Colonel Adams what Ycnan Snave had said, they also told him about the human researchers offer to help in any way they could, Colonel Adams then said, do you mind if I make a suggestion? Please do, replied Yikem, right then, said the Colonel, I think the best thing you can do is send one of your associates that you trust to speak to the researchers, and find out just how willing they are to help.

And to tell them that there's a good chance of them getting hurt, or even killed if they get caught, that way you'll know for certain if they are genuine or not. In the meantime, we need to find a way of getting you and the rest of the F T W ambassadors out of here, as soon as possible, because we are not that far from Hereford where the SAS are based. Now I expect the F T W have heard of the SAS. However, just in case you haven't, let me just tell you that they are the best soldiers in the world, and if they're on your case then you really do have a major problem, because these guys will not stop until they complete the mission.

Colonel Adams knew this to be true because he was an officer in the SAS for ten years, until he had to leave, due to an unfortunate accident when his parachute failed to open, and he ended up "landing" in a small woodland that was luckily full of young saplings that broke his fall. (Along with most of the bones in his body) and thereby saving his life.

And although he sustained some serious injuries, he did make near enough a full recovery, and Major Toby Fry who was also serving in the SAS was with him on the day of his accident. (He was also responsible for saving the Colonels life) and that's how they became lifelong friends.

Although the Colonel never mentioned any of this to the F T W but not because he had something to hide, it just didn't seem relevant enough for him to mention it to them. So, he knew exactly what the SAS were capable of, so he said I must emphasise the importance of getting all of you out of here, and as soon as possible.

Now the F T W had a total of eight representatives (including Yikem and Eigroeg,) and it was decided to ask the remaining six if two of them would be willing to pose as Yikem and Eigroeg. While the other four just behaved as naturally as they could when they boarded the helicopter that was meant to take them to Cardiff Airport and the start of their long journey back to their jungle home.

(That's if the pilot doesn't notice that the F T W was missing two Ambassadors, which the Colonel thought to be highly unlikely,) and he would also mention before anyone steps forward that the British Government intends to destroy the helicopter in mid-air.

However, the good news is the F T W, as we speak are destroying every weapon that exists, along with disabling or destroying every submarine, battleship, tank, plane, and helicopter, so there is a very good chance we may just about get away with it. But obviously, we can't risk putting Yikem or Eigroeg on that flight just in case the SAS have already been assigned to do the job, in which case they are probably already out there waiting for you.

And that's when Eigroeg said to her team, now I know you all have families to go home to, so please, I don't want anyone to feel obligated or pressured in any way to volunteer, because we would completely understand if no one's willing to take the risk. And we would just devise another plan, so, as I said, there's absolutely no obligation, and no one would hold it against any of you, and I promise you have my word on that.

So, the question was finally asked, and every member of the F T W stepped forward (including Yikem and Eigroeg) so Colonel Adams suggested that he should be the one to Choose the two volunteers, simply because he knew nothing about any of them. So, he wouldn't be swayed either way by the fact that some of them had young families to go home to and some didn't.

And so, it was agreed, the Colonel eventually selected the two most likely candidates based on their height, build, and weight. (Which resulted in Eigroeg complaining vigorously about her replacement, because she refused to believe they were the same size, and she remained adamant that she was at least one, but more than likely two, sizes smaller than her stand in.) And then Yikem's aide Igoy stepped forward and asked if he could be the one to talk to the researchers that offered to help, and to find out if they had any suggestions.

At that point, Colonel Adams said that was a good idea, but obviously, no one outside the present company in this room must know of his involvement in any of this, because he would be a much better asset in helping the F T W if he was working from the inside.

He then gave his word that he was now one hundred percent behind the F T W and would do as much as he possibly could to help them win this war against his species. And much to the Colonels surprise, not one single member of the F T W doubted him, this also included every animal and insect in the world that was listening intently to the conversation.

So, the Colonel was now officially, an unofficial member of the F T W (if that makes sense,) however, while they'd been sorting everything out, the F T W were also very busy all over the world, destroying anything. and everything, that could even vaguely be used as a weapon, along with anything else that may have been useful to mankind.

The electricity, gas, and water supply to every hospital worldwide had now been shut down. All the weapons had either been destroyed or were damaged beyond repair; the humans had noticed that most of their fuel reserves had gone missing and decided the best thing to do was to put all the remaining fuel into whatever needed it. (Which is exactly what the F T W had hoped they'd do, because as I said it had been contaminated with finely powdered glass) and much to the delight of the F T W, within minutes of them starting the engines they just ground to a halt and had seized solid, so were now nothing more than expensive pieces of scrap metal.

Yikem and Eigroeg informed the Colonel of what had been happening worldwide, the Colonel just smiled and asked if the telephone could be turned on, as he believed now would be an ideal time to ring the prime minister and catch him off guard. So, the phones were once more reconnected, and the call was made, then after a few short minutes, the phone was answered.

However, it was answered by the prime minister's personal secretary, whose name was Les Adams and before Colonel Adams had a chance to speak, the private secretary said, I do apologize but the prime minister is extremely busy at the moment, and could you please ring back later, or if you prefer, I could take a message? So, the Colonel replied yes, I would like to leave a message. Could you please inform the prime minister that Colonel Adams rang to confirm that I have received his message and will be awaiting further instruction from him, preferably as soon as possible.

The private secretary then replied how she would give the prime minister the message as soon as she had a chance to do so. The Colonel said thank you to the personal secretary and then added, I hope whatever the prime minister is busy dealing with is nothing too serious, he thanked her once more for her time and put the phone down.

He then turned to face Yikem and Eigroeg with a huge smile on his face, and said oh, I think you've got him in a bit of a flap now, which hopefully we can use to our advantage. So, all we can do for the time being is wait for the prime minister to get in touch. In the meantime,

Yikem, if you could get your aide Igoy to talk to the researchers that offered to help, and let's see if they come up with any good ideas.

So Igoy was called into the meeting room and was asked if he was still willing to talk to the researchers? And how he was under no obligation whatsoever to do so, and if he had changed his mind, it would be okay. However, Igoy practically demanded that he should be the one to speak on behalf of the F T W, so everyone agreed, and Igoy promptly went to look for the researchers.

And fifteen minutes later Igoy and the two researchers were sat in a quiet office away from prying eyes, and Igoy started to explain how the F T W needed a backup plan just in case they needed to get the representatives out of the fallout shelter quickly, and more importantly undetected.

(Because Igoy had decided not to tell them the full story just in case they were spies.)

However, Igoy did go slightly over the top by emphasising the dangers of what could happen if they were caught helping the F T W, and Igoy watched every single move and twitch they made as he explained in great detail, what the possible consequences could be as a result of them helping the F T W, especially when he told them how they would more than probably be tortured, and or killed by the armed forces for even offering to help them.

Igoy was beginning to relish his role as a storyteller and was now starting to become a little over excited and thought sod it, let's go for gold.

So, he decided to drop the bombshell, by telling them that if they agreed to help but then decided to double cross them, the F T W would not only kill them, but also their entire families. (Which definitely hit a nerve and visibly shook the researchers) and Igoy was now thinking oh shit, I've really screwed it up now.

But much to his surprise, (and very much to his relief) the researchers still wanted to help, they both quickly swore their allegiance to the F T W, and Igoy could tell they genuinely meant every word they said. So, he now decided it was time to tell them the truth.

However, he did emphasise that the risk of them being killed by the armed forces for helping them was a very genuine one. To which the researchers replied they were more than willing to put their lives on the line to help save the planet and its inhabitants (which I must admit impressed Igoy, the F T W and myself enormously,) so a few suggestions were put forward by the researchers.

One idea put forward was to simply hide them in the back of a car, van or lorry and drive them straight out through the main gates. Then the other researcher (very seriously) suggested killing everyone in the place, except of course the helicopter pilot and flying them straight back to their jungle home. Which to be honest the F T W thought was a bit on the drastic side, and they found the whole idea rather disconcerting, to say the least, and also very typical of mankind who appear to think that destroying and/or killing something is the solution to all their problems, plus a much tamer version of the helicopter idea had already been put forward.

However, the helicopter's fuel tanks wouldn't hold anywhere near enough fuel to get them home without stopping somewhere to refuel, although, it hadn't been completely ruled out. Because the F T W knew where all the top-secret army, navy, and air force bases were, worldwide. They also knew how much fuel reserves were in each base.

The F T W decided they had no other choice but to keep the researcher on their side (either that or kill him) which they didn't really want to do, so Igoy suggested that he would put these proposals forward to his superiors for consideration. He thanked the researchers for their time and commitment, he then added, as soon as I get a reply from my superiors, I will let you know their decision.

He also reminded them that they obviously couldn't discuss what they've spoken about to anyone, no matter how much they trusted them. And how Igoy would personally vet any new supporters that came forward, and both researchers excitedly and simultaneously blurted out we'll get the names and addresses for you to look at, and that's when Igoy really lost his temper. and shouted, haven't you listened to anything I've just said about not discussing what we have talked about here today? And I will tell you one thing for nothing.

And that is, if you introduce someone who can't keep their mouths shut, and tell "outsiders" what we are planning, or possibly even be a spy, then the person that put their name forward will personally be held responsible and will be punished accordingly.

And you have my word that it will not, be a pleasant experience, because the F T W will not tolerate under any circumstances anyone that puts them, or any of its supporters at risk in any way whatsoever, do I make myself clear?

Both researchers replied (rather sheepishly) yes sir, you have sir, and we can only apologize for appearing a bit too keen, but we really do want to help in any way we can, and we only have four names to put forward because it was their idea to offer to help in the first place.

Igoy replied fair enough, but you must realize just how important secrecy is to the F T W, and please don't call me sir, my name is Igoy, and I would be grateful if you didn't reveal that to anyone.

The researchers then promised that they wouldn't tell anyone anything, until he had finished vetting them. And with that, Igoy once again thanked them for their time, and said we will continue this discussion in the morning, and just as he started to walk away, he stopped and asked them how security conscious the guards on the gate were? And how often did they stop and search any vehicles entering or leaving the premises? To which the researchers replied, they normally inspect incoming Lorries and cars, but once they get to know the drivers then they very rarely checked them on the way in or out.

Igoy thought to himself well that could be a possible way of getting Yikem and Eigroeg out of the complex, and with that he once again (and definitely for the last time) said goodbye to the researchers, and left to go and find Yikem, Eigroeg, and Colonel Adams to find out if the prime minister had been in touch.

Because so as not to be distracted he had "turned down" which meant he could be heard, but he wouldn't "receive" anything while talking to the researchers whose names are Robert and Gareth Williams.

He immediately "turned back up" once he had left the researchers. He eventually, much to his surprise, found the Colonel, Yikem, and Eigroeg still sat in the meeting room where he had left them several hours earlier, so he explained what had been said. (Just for the Colonels benefit) because obviously Yikem and Eigroeg already knew, and the Colonel appeared to be very interested in the fact that the guards on the gate were a bit complacent about stopping and searching traffic if they recognized either the driver or the passengers.

He was also a bit concerned about the one researcher who planned to kill everyone except the helicopter pilot. And decided they should all keep a very close watch on him, and maybe it would be a good idea to pull his medical records to see if he had any ongoing psychological problems, they should know about.

Yikem then instructed a couple of flies to accompany the researchers at all times, and how they had to monitor who they talked to, what they talked about, where they went, and so on, to find out if they could be trusted. And, to find out if their offer to help the F T W was indeed a genuine one.

Although Igoy seemed certain the researchers meant what they said, however, he did agree with the Colonels sentiment that it was better to be safe than sorry. Plus, once the flies have reported back to Yikem where the researchers live then he could send a few spiders, along with some fleas and bedbugs that were small enough to be practically invisible into their homes, to watch and listen to what was being said or planned.

The Colonel agreed it was a good idea, he also commented on how the F T W still managed to surprise him by just how well organized they were, and how they always seem capable of anticipating mankind's next move well in advance (with a few exceptions) as if they know how mankind thought.

And then the phone rang. Colonel Adams just sat there, leaving it to ring for a while, (not wanting to appear over keen,) eventually, he picked it up, and sure enough it was the prime minister who, once again was in a foul mood, so the Colonel said (rather sarcastically) hello prime minister, and thank you for ringing back.

To which the prime minister replied, this had better be important Colonel, as I have rather a lot on my plate at the moment, because the F T W have now turned off all the power in the hospitals, along with the house of lords, the house of commons, Buckingham palace and any other important building, including every politician's home in the country (including the prime minister's home) which he was not at all happy about, as he had only just had all the electric's in number ten repaired after the visit (and I quote) from them bloody fire ants.

He then added, and the bloody things are still in the house, they have now also developed a very nasty habit of sneaking out at night when we are asleep, and biting us just to remind us, they are still here.

I've had pest control experts in, and even they can't find them. But something must be done because the bites hurt like hell, and no-one's had a decent night's sleep for over a week, and it's now beginning to have an effect on our concentration (And our tempers,) which really isn't doing me any favours at all at the moment, considering what's going on all over the world.

To which the Colonel innocently replied, well I wouldn't know sir, due to the fact the F T W only turn the phones back on when I gave them a plausible reason, and even then, they monitor every conversation. However, they have now agreed that it's in everybody's best interests to leave this line permanently connected.

Anyway, if you don't mind sir, I'd like to get back to the reason I called, because as I said I can only imagine how busy you must be now, plus, when I spoke to your personal secretary, I got the feeling things weren't quite going the way you expected. I just thought I'd let you know how things are progressing here.

Well, the truth of the matter is we are making progress, slowly but surely, although they are not too willing to compromise on many things, and to be honest with your sir, they seem to be a lot more intelligent, and definitely a lot more organized than we originally gave them credit for, and they know exactly what they want, and more importantly they also know exactly how to get it.

The prime minister replied I already know that, because the F T W. have now either disabled, or destroyed all of our weapons and machinery worldwide, including every naval ship and submarine, and also every military plane, tank, and lorry, because someone, and although we can't prove it, we are assuming it was the work of the F T W have polluted all of our fuel reserves with what appears to be very finely powdered glass, and now every machine or vehicle we've put it in has seized solid and is now as good as beyond repair. Because the same can be said for all the machinery needed to make any repairs, so we really are pretty much screwed, so I think the best thing to do for the time being is to keep them with you, and to persevere with the talks, and try to come to some mutually beneficial agreement.

The message once decoded meant just keep them where they are, so they can't go anywhere just in case we need to use them in some sort of bargaining strategy, to which the colonel replied, that sounds like a good idea sir, and if there are any new developments then I will inform you immediately.

The prime minister then replied, thank you Colonel Adams, and if you can pull this off then I can personally, guarantee there will be a big promotion in it for you.

The Colonel was in the process of saying thank you, when he was interrupted by the prime minister saying, sorry Colonel I must go, because I have the president of the United States on the other line. (Because the F T W had agreed that all the world leader's telephones would remain connected for them to communicate with each other as they attempt to work out a deal with the F T W.) So, colonel if you could please keep me informed as much as possible, I would be most grateful, and then he hung up.

So, Colonel Adams was happy with the fact they now had more time to come up with a plan to get Yikem, Eigroeg, and company safely out of the research Centre, and hopefully back to the relative safety of their jungle home.

Plus, the Colonel now new for certain that the SAS were not outside waiting for them, as the prime minister would most certainly have mentioned it if they were, which was really good news indeed, as it now gave them some much-needed breathing space. And that was pretty much the end of another day, so everyone said goodnight to each other, and went off for some much needed and well-earned rest.

Within ten minutes of Yikem entering his quarters there was a knock on his door, and once told to enter in walked Igoy, who asked Yikem if he would be requiring anything before, he retired for the evening? Yikem replied no thank you Igoy, I'm fine thank you. Now go and relax as you've had quite an eventful day, and I must admit I was very impressed with how well you handled your meeting with the researchers today. And I will also admit to singing your praises to Ycnan Snave so thank you once again.

But instead of leaving, Igoy just stood there fidgeting, so Yikem asked him if there was anything wrong? and was there anything he could do for him? Igoy replied, might I ask you a question please sir? Yikem immediately replied, of course, you can, but only on the condition, you no longer call me sir. For two very simple reasons, the first one being I never have, or ever will, like anyone calling me sir, plus we only agreed to do this servant thing to get the humans thinking we were more like them.

And secondly, ever since we were little, I have always classed you as my equal, and more importantly to me; right the way through our childhood and into adulthood you have always been my very good, loyal, and trustworthy friend. Which means a great deal to me personally, and I think the world would be a much better, and certainly a much happier place to live in if there were more apes like you in it.

Right then, that's that out of the way, so what was it you wanted to talk to me about? And Igoy, who was still somewhat shocked by the openness of Yikem's last statement just had to sit down in the chair that was thankfully directly behind him because his legs just buckled.

Then Igoy looked up at Yikem with a somewhat worried look on his face, and he asked this question, could you please answer me truthfully...... Do you really believe we will get out of here alive? And do you honestly think we will ever make it back home to our families and friends?

Yikem, rather surprised by Igoy's question, (which by the look on his face had obviously been bothering him for quite some time,) so he went over and sat down next to him, and replied reassuringly well of course I do, why? Don't you think we'll make it?

Igoy replied well I really would like to think we will, but you have to admit we are stuck in some strange country, thousands of miles from home, surrounded by people we don't know, plus most of them just want to kill us, so the odds of us making it home are very much stacked up against us, don't you think so?

However, before Yikem could answer him, there was another knock at the door and Yikem said to Igoy well aren't I, the popular one tonight, (in an attempt to lighten the mood.)

However, Igoy automatically stood up, and was about to walk over to open the door when Yikem told him to sit back down as he would see who was there, and when he opened the door Eigroeg was stood there because she had picked up their conversation and thought she would also try to help put Igoy's mind at rest.

So, she was invited in, and Igoy once again stood up and was again told to sit down, this time by Eigroeg, who went and sat next to him, and as she put her arm around his shoulders, she told him how she was also missing her family and friends.

She also told him how she was very determined to see them all again, hopefully in the not-too-distant future, because she fully intended to be alive to tell her children and her yet unborn grandchildren the story of how they had overthrown mankind and saved the world, along with all its occupants from certain destruction.

She then explained to Igoy that mankind really didn't stand a chance of winning this fight, because we can outsmart and outthink them, plus, at the moment, they are too busy killing each other to worry about us, and they have no food, very little water, no way of keeping warm and nowhere to live.

So, believe me, we will beat them one-way or another, and it is now entirely up to them to decide whether they want to do it the easy, or the hard way. However, I honestly believe mankind, purely through their sheer arrogance, along with the misplaced belief that they really are the "superior beings" on this planet, they will instinctively choose the hard way.

Because the main problem that mankind suffers from is their blind conviction that they are invincible and can quite easily win this war because they truly, (and vainly,) believe they really do know the answers to everything.

Combined with the fact that they also believe the only way to do something is to do it their way, without questioning the reasoning. And that's why this planet is in such a mess, this is also the reason we had no other choice but to intervene. Because if humanity had decided to stop destroying everyone's home and stopped the pollution along with the needless destruction of the rainforests, which are this planet's lungs, then we wouldn't have needed to get involved.

Because as you know we were quite happily getting on with our lives until mankind became too greedy, in his constant need to make, and increase, his profits, no matter what the cost, even to the point of destroying the most important thing of all. Which is, of course the planet. Along with everything that lives here.

And they need to realise that everything on this planet including mankind, is in one way or another inextricably linked, and therefore are very much dependent on each other for their very survival. And how the crucial balance between all life forms must, at all costs remain stable, if we are to have any chance of surviving, sadly the most important thing to humanity appears to be the constant, and overwhelming desire for a bigger and bigger profit.

We all know that it's practically impossible to tell them anything. And unfortunately, the only way we can hope to get this message across to them is going to be through the huge amount of life that will be lost both to mankind and animal kind alike during this war, which I think is a very sad thing, as we have no desire to kill, or destroy anything. But we have now run out of all other options such as massive oil spills, or gas and oil rigs' bursting into flames.

Yes, that was us. (Well actually, it was our associates) Who were trying to frighten humanity to its senses in an attempt to scare them into realizing the error of their ways, but to no avail, so here we are, the last hope, as it's now down to us to stop mankind before it's too late to save our planet.

And this time, the battle will literally be fought to the death, because if we don't fight all of us will die, but if we do fight then some of us will live, which admittedly seems a high price to pay, however, the majority (hopefully on both sides) will survive. So, it all quite simply boils down to humanity either coming to its senses or becoming extinct.

And unfortunately for them, they are the only ones that can make that choice and decide their fate. And as I said, I think we all know which one they will choose, so unfortunately even though we have an ace up our sleeve, I still believe this war will go on for quite some time, and at a huge cost to both the planet and its inhabitants.

And that's when an eerie silence descended on the room as they all suddenly realized just how serious the situation had become. Because although they knew what was happening all over the world, I don't really think the severity of it all had fully sunk in, until now.

As many of them including Yikem Snave, had gone to this meeting treating it as a bit of an adventure, and a holiday, convinced that everything would be sorted out within a couple of days, maybe a week at the most, then they would all return home, and just be able to get on with their lives without having to worry about poacher's traps, or illegal loggers cutting down the forests around them.

So now, the penny had truly dropped, so to speak, as the full reality of what was happening finally hit them like a ton of bricks. And they were left speechless as each one of them found their own way to come to terms with it all.

And while they were all having a moment's contemplation the outside world had gone crazy, because word had somehow gotten out about the destruction of all humanity's weapons. As the news spread, huge gangs of people started descending on the Houses of Parliament. Demanding to know why they hadn't been told the truth about what's really going on, and why were the Houses of Parliament along with every politician's home (including their second homes) still connected to all the main services, while ordinary people were struggling to keep warm, with very little food, water or shelter?

The security forces were doing the best they could to control the situation; however, the huge mob of people knew the only protection the guards had were riot shields and batons, plus the guards were outnumbered by a minimum of fifty to one.

So even if the guards had still had automatic weapons, I don't really think it would have made any difference whatsoever, because these people had decided they'd had enough of the politicians getting everything they wanted, while, as usual, the general public suffered. So, the prime minister got to his feet and tried his best to explain that the F T W had disconnected all the main services two days ago.

He then went waffling on about "how we are all in this together" when for some unknown reason one of the protesters tried the light switch and lo and behold, the light came on. So, the prime minister was called a pompous conceited liar (or words to that effect) then all hell let loose, because apparently, (although reports are a bit on the sketchy side) at least four politicians were beaten to death, and a large number of them were seriously injured by the angry crowd, and things were now completely out of control as anarchy took over.

And that's when the prime minister realized just how devious, and cunning the F T W could be, because the electricity along with everything else, had indeed been turned off a few days earlier, so the F T W must have known what was going on and turned all the services back on, just to make the politicians look like liars. (Although they don't really need any help in that department.)

Eventually, after a few more hours of chaos, the crowds started to lose momentum, and people started wandering off, bored of it all, and only once everyone had gone was the full carnage realized, because the once sumptuous building now looked more like a bomb site.

However, that was the least of their problems, because the F T W had been monitoring the riot and was quite pleased with the "fruits of their labour" because it was obvious, they had set the whole thing up, with the sole intention of turning the public against the politicians. Because in reality it's the governments of this world along with the big ridiculously rich companies, (which rule the governments,) are the ones responsible for causing most, if not all, of this planet's problems.

The F T W had also taken note on how the protesters were angry about how the politicians had everything while they were struggling to survive. Therefore, the F T W decided it was time to put stage two of the plan into operation.

And to make amends the F T W reconnected the power supply (as it came from a renewable source) to the homes of the "common people" so they issued the order to return the homes to their rightful owners; however, the shops and offices would remain occupied.

And as a few politicians and members of staff were attempting to assess the damage done to this once opulent building, they became the first people to witness what stage two of the plan meant, because the "vermin" that once occupied people's homes had now been told that the parliamentary buildings, along with all politician's homes (including number ten Downing Street) would make ideal replacements.

So, they were now entering the buildings in colossal numbers, and at an incredible speed, and the noise they made on their approach into the Houses of parliament (which sounded like heavy rain on a tin roof) could be heard for several minutes before anyone caught sight of its source.

Although a few people had a fairly good idea of what was coming at them, because they had heard that dreadful sound once before. It was the day the "vermin" first descended on London.

Those that recognized the sound were already running for the nearest fire exits, while shouting run for your lives, at their colleagues, that were just stood there staring at each other completely confused, because they knew whatever was making this horrendous sound was bad.

They also fully understood how they should follow their colleague's advice and run for the exits. However, curiosity was compelling them to stay, to discover what was making the strange sound, which had now become so loud that it hurt their ears. Then suddenly just as their fleeing, advice giving associates finally managed to fumble the fire doors open, curiosity was satisfied, as a tidal wave of vermin, over two metres high burst into the huge room, and in a matter of seconds had completely engulfed and destroyed everything and anyone that stood in their path, including those by the fire doors.

And several days later when the autopsy reports for the eighty-four unfortunate people that died that day were finally released, the cause of death was put down to suffocation, because apparently, the vermin were so "tightly packed" that the people just couldn't breathe.

However, these people were not crushed to death, because according to a memo written by a Doctor David (Dai) Steed, who was the coroner that performed the postmortems, stated how these people had technically been drowned by the sheer volume of rats alone.

So now, the once opulent House of Lords along with the House of Commons had been reduced to nothing more than a mere shell. Consisting of just four walls and some remnants of a roof, because the huge joists that had once supported the upper floors in these buildings had quite simply snapped like a dry twig beneath the incredible weight that had so suddenly been placed upon them.

However, every politician in the country had enough problems of his or her own to contend with, because during the takeover of the Parliamentary buildings every politician and wealthy businessperson in the country was also undergoing the same fate and had no other choice but to abandon their home.

(Or should I say both homes) as vermin overran them, and now this strange twist of fate (that the F T W had meticulously orchestrated) the table had been turned, because every politician and wealthy businessperson in the country were now homeless, with no food or shelter.

Forced to wander the streets, watching members of the public walking back into their now vermin free homes. And having to listen to the squeals of delight coming from the small children as they realised, they now not only had somewhere to live, but they also had free electricity and heating.

For a short time, even the Queen of England herself was homeless. (For eighteen weeks) which seemed like a lifetime to her, and her family. However, that was only done to prove a point, which was how no one was beyond the reach of the F T W.

So now, there was no doubt whatsoever in the "people of powers" minds that they were no longer in control of anything, because within minutes they'd gone from extremely wealthy and highly influential people to mere Homeless Street beggars that no one would acknowledge or help.

This, in turn, had created a completely new, and very frightening world for the once influential people who had never wanted for anything in their lives. Because they didn't have the vaguest idea of what to do, where to go, or how they were going to fend for themselves, instead of getting someone else to do it for them, or simply ordering it in.

And within hours the general public were taking a great deal of pleasure from taunting and teasing these once important people, as they watched them desperately rummaging through the piles of rubbish that now littered the streets in a desperate attempt to find something to eat.

Some were so desperate that they were trying to swap their expensive Rolex watches and jewellery for food and shelter. However, all they received for their pleading was a severe beating, and being robbed of everything they had, then getting told how they were welcome to life in the real world.

One well-known Member of Parliament, who was personally responsible for many of the public expenditure cutbacks that has caused so much grief and hardship for these people, (especially the disabled and the homeless) was now stood in the centre of the street demanding, at the top of his voice, how he and his family should immediately be taken into someone's home and looked after, on the grounds of whom he was, and how on many occasions he had gone "out of his way" to help these people so many times in the past.

However, the reply wasn't quite what he expected because all he received was abuse, and smart-arse remarks from the people who had suffered greatly due to his so-called help.

So now, like the pompous ass that he was, he started shouting do you know who I am, and how dare you defy me. Along with threats of how he would make them all suffer once he was back in power, whilst flailing his arms, and stamping his feet, like a spoilt child in full swing of throwing a huge tantrum at the now laughing crowd that had gathered to look at this familiar looking clown that was stood in the street entertaining the people.

Many of which were relishing the chance to get their own back and were making some, shall we say, rather unflattering comments, just to get him even more angry in order to keep the free entertainment going for as long as possible, because let's face it, there wasn't much else to watch.

Plus, it really was extremely funny watching a fully-grown, well-educated man, stood in the street throwing a major tantrum in a really posh voice.

This tantrum had now been going on for the best part of two hours, and bets that would be paid for with food or useful items, were now being placed on how long they could keep him going, and the lucky person that got the closest time would win himself or herself a lovely top of the range Rolex wristwatch.

Oh yes indeed, some are born businesspeople, and this one was a wandering "trader" that just happened to be passing through, he was known by the name of Pancho, he also had a natural talent for spotting an opportunity, and quickly realised that if he worked this crowd correctly, he stood to make a nice little profit.

Because all the stuff he received as payment for the bets he'd then use to barter for other things, whereas he would never be able to do the same with the Rolex, simply because it was now nothing more than a pretty trinket.

Plus, as Pancho had a bit of a tendency to travel around quite a bit, the chances of him still being in town for long after the entertainment had finished were very slim.

Because as soon as he'd collected his dues, he'd be off before all the excitement had died down, and the lucky winner realizing that the prize (that's if they were fortunate enough to get it off Pancho) they had paid so dearly for in the heat of the moment was in fact worthless, as it now served no purpose, because no one needed to know the exact time anymore. So true to form as four hours later the politicians constant shouting had reduced his voice to a hoarse whisper, Pancho was busily walking amongst the crowd collecting his dues, knowing full well he would have to leave some of the forfeited bets behind, but that was okay because the large van he was driving (which he'd won in a bet) had been converted to run on batteries and had a large solar panel fitted to the roof.

The van was now packed full of goodies, and he would soon be off on his travels, so he was doing his utmost to whip his audience into a betting frenzy by shouting how long do you think he'll continue, ten minutes, half an hour maybe? Come on, place your bets before it's too late to become the owner of this top-notch Rolex watch.

He then causes an argument between two people which then turned into a huge fight, thereby giving Pancho several minutes to get in his van and sneak off to the next town.

And as he drove away, he congratulated himself on what a good day's business he's had, then looking at his wrist and thinking to himself how the Rolex really suited him, and how it looked like it belonged there, never giving so much as a second thought to the people he'd conned, and the trouble he'd caused, and of course every country has at least one of its own versions of Pancho.

Meanwhile back in Builth Wells, the escape plan for the F T W delegates had progressed, as both Ycnan and Haras Snave had been busily going through every available option, and they had come to the conclusion that the best way to get Yikem Snave and associates' home was to use the helicopter they'd arrived at the meeting in to fly them to France, where the human supporters would have a plane ready to fly them directly to Africa where transport back to their home would be waiting.

Now obviously they couldn't use the original pilot to fly them out as they were hoping that (with a bit of careful planning) no one would notice them missing for at least a couple of days, thereby giving them a good head start.

Now while Ycnan and Haras Snave were in the final stage of the escape plan, Igoy had already asked the human supporters, who had now been abbreviated by the F T W to the F T W S (Free the World Supporters) if they had anyone capable of flying the large Chinook helicopter? And a few hours later the F T W S (with great delight) reported back to Igoy that they had just the man for the job, his name was David (Dai) Merlin Davies (he earned the nickname Merlin because he was a Welshman that was a "wizard" at building custom motorcycles and trikes) he was an ex RAF Chinook pilot that had been discharged from the RAF for being "a bit of a wild one" however the RAF had unofficially admitted that he was the best Chinook pilot they had, but unfortunately, he had to go because they just couldn't control him.

So, Dai Merlin was asked if he would be willing to accept this mission, which could quite easily cost him his life, and as far as he knew his only reward would be nothing more than the gratitude of the F T W. However, Dai being Dai jumped at the chance of getting back into a Chinook again, regardless of the dangers.

But he did stipulate there would be one condition, which was, it would have to be done his way, with no interference from anyone. He would work out the route, along with any and everything else that was to do with the mission.

He then said I have one more condition (which was more of a request than a demand really) because all he had to say was do you think I could keep the Chinook once I get you lot back to your home, please?

The F T W just stood there, somewhat confused, as to why he'd want to keep it. Then whilst looking up at the ceiling with his hand supporting his chin Dai added (as an afterthought) oh, and I'm going to need free aviation fuel for the rest of my life. Then, as if to justify his last request he added, well it's no good me having it if I can't fly the bloody thing is it, which when you think about it does make sense.

Yikem and Eigroeg considered his requests for several minutes before agreeing to meet his terms, on the condition that he never used the Chinook against them. And how the Aviation fuel was for his own personal use only, plus he had to realize that the aviation fuel would eventually run out, and if they ever discovered he was either selling, or trading it they would stop his supply immediately, they would also destroy his beloved Chinook.

Dai (still struggling to contain his excitement) explained to the F T W how he had already sworn his allegiance to them, long before this escape plan had been devised. He then explained how he was not happy with the thought that his loyalty was in any way under question, and if they weren't one hundred per cent certain of his commitment then he would leave, swearing never to tell another living soul about what they'd discussed in this room.

Yikem and Eigroeg immediately apologized for doubting him, to which Dai (whilst rubbing his hands together in unconcealed delight) replied, so I can keep the Chinook then? And that's when the F T W fully realized what the phrase "a bit of a wild one" really meant, because they had finally realized that Dai was a loyal and trustworthy supporter, but he was also very much his own man, who had absolutely no interest whatsoever in conforming to anyone's so-called standards, and from that day on he was treated with great respect by the F T W.

It was now 0.200 hrs. so the meeting was called to an end with Dai having the last word. Saying he would start planning the mission immediately, and how he would be in touch as soon as it was ready.

In the meantime, the Fire ants had been busy, constantly annoying the prime minister and his family whenever they tried to sleep, so the relationship between the family and staff was now close to breaking point, due to the never-ending arguments that seemed to start over nothing in particular, and went on for hours, thereby draining their already exhausted minds and bodies of what little energy they had left, and they were now close to turning into twitching gibbering wrecks.

The F T W were being constantly updated and had instructed the fire ants to keep the pressure on the family, to keep them so preoccupied with the problem that the prime minister wouldn't be thinking of anything else, giving the F T W much needed breathing space to finalise their plan.

Four days later Dai Merlin Davies gets in touch, asking for a meeting with Yikem and Eigroeg, which was then arranged for 10.00 hours the following morning. One of the F T W S was given a security clearance pass to give to Dai, which had his name on, and stated he was a "highly classified" maintenance operative with full security clearance, which enabled him to go anywhere without question, which technically meant he had more authority than Colonel Adams.

Dai, however, didn't realise this, until every soldier in the place started standing to attention and saluting him every time he walked by, so he spent the next twenty minutes strutting about, showing his pass to everyone, and loving every minute of it, until one of the F T W S who'd been sent to find him, told him it was time for the meeting and off they went.

Yikem, Eigroeg, Igoy, and Colonel Adams were all sat in the meeting room when Dai arrived, and after saying a quick hello to everyone, he decided to get straight down to business.

So, with a big mug of coffee in his hand he pulled back a chair, sat down, had a big slurp of his coffee, and started to explain his "plan of action." He started with all the possible route's they could take, including the good and bad points of using each one.

The first of which was the most obvious one, Paris, which meant once the military discovered the F T W representatives were missing, it would be the first place they would look.

Dai went on to suggest going straight to Portugal, then into either Libya, or Algeria, and eventually to the border between Chad and Niger. Dai then asked if anyone had any objections, comments, or suggestions they'd like to make, then now would be the time to do so, then after taking another big swig of his coffee he leaned back in his chair, anticipating a barrage of questions, and objections, however, after a few moments of silence with everybody just sat in their chairs looking blankly at each other, Colonel Adams asked Yikem and Eigroeg Snave if they had any preference, or any questions they'd like to ask Dai?

To which Yikem replied, well, we were all talking about various routes home, and the same route was mentioned several times, so I think the best option is Portugal, then through Libya, as it seems by what Dai said, it would be the least obvious route, and hopefully the military will look at the most likely ways first, which with a bit of luck would mean we would be back home on our mountain long before they worked it out.

And so, it was decided, this was the way they'd go. So now all they had to do was work out a story to tell the helicopter pilot, and where they could refuel without too many awkward questions being asked, but to be honest the refuelling shouldn't be too much of a problem, plus they already had a plausible (ish) reason to give the pilot.

So, the only thing left to do now was working out where to refuel, and when would be the best time to put the plan into action. Yikem Snave contacted Ycnan and Haras Snave to confirm the route they would be taking.

A few weeks later, once they'd finalised the plan then checked, and double checked the route and refuelling stops. they decided they would leave on the Thursday evening at 19.00 hours. They had also decided that the best way to deal with the pilot was to lace his food with Valium thereby making him dopey and disorientated.

The intention being to then arrest him for being drunk on duty and locking him up in a secure room for seven days of solitary confinement as punishment.

Yikem Snave almost felt sorry for the pilot as he tried to argue his case (in a very slurred voice whilst wobbling all over the place) that there was no way on earth he would even think about drinking on duty, he also tried to explain how he had fourteen years of unblemished service to his name, which he would be most grateful if Colonel Adams could take into account before reporting him to his superiors.

Eventually when the Colonel stopped shouting at him, the pilot was then told that the Colonel would not report him for his misconduct, but he would have no choice but to lock him up as an example to the other men. The pilot agreed with the Colonel, although he still swore blind how he hadn't touched a drop of alcohol, but he would accept his punishment.

He then thanked the Colonel for his leniency, which the Colonel found very heart-warming (and very comical as the pilot was wobbling all over the place and now had a fit of the giggles.)

So, the Colonel raised his voice once more as he commanded the pilot to pull yourself together man, you are an embarrassment to yourself, and your uniform. The Colonel then ordered the guards to take him away.

The pilot (still giggling like a little schoolgirl) slurred, I do apologise most sincerely Colonel, and whilst still strongly denying he'd been drinking wobbled off out through the door, bouncing off the doorframe as he went with the guards following behind doing their utmost to keep a straight face (but failing dismally,) so just for good measure the Colonel barked an order at them to sort themselves out, or they'd be joining the pilot in solitary, which soon wiped the grins off their faces.

Once they'd left the Colonel remarked, I didn't like doing that one little bit, I've just publicly humiliated a damn good pilot, and a highly respected person. Maybe one day I'll get the chance to apologise to the man whose name was Mike Cannon. Who, unbeknown to the F T W would have quite happily flown the helicopter for them, as he secretly agreed with what the F T W were doing, his sister Valerie (Bobby) Cannon and his nephew Grant Cannon were both members of the F T W S.

So Thursday arrived, and everyone was ready, Dai arrived at 13.00 hours to double check everything and to have a final run-through of the plan, at 16.00 Yikem, Eigroeg and associates received their final briefing, and asked if anyone had any questions they wanted to ask, or if there was anything they weren't sure about then this was the time to say, and it would be explained to them, as it was very important that every one of them understood the role they'd play or the plan could fail. No one had any questions, and all of them said they knew what they had to do.

19.00 hours arrived, and they all gingerly walked out to the chinook helicopter just as Dai was running his final checks before starting her up, Dai then (a little excitedly) asked them to board.

Colonel Adams had escorted the entourage under armed guard to the Chinook and just as they boarded, he said to Yikem Snave to talk to his superiors about what they had discussed, and could he please inform the Colonel of any decision they came too. He then thanked them for their time, effort, and commitment to resolving this issue.

He and the armed escort then stood to attention, about turned, saluted, and marched away.

Dai Merlin Davies waited until the Colonel and the escort were well out of the way before starting his Chinook, and that was it, they were away up into the air and gone, everything had gone as smooth as silk.

Yet Yikem Snave and co were just sat very quietly, staring at the floor, as Dai took great pleasure in explaining what the chinook could and couldn't do, he really loved these machines, and you could literally ask him anything from the top speed to what thread and what size bolt held the rotor on and you could put money on him knowing the right answer.

Dai in his excitement never noticed that not one of his passengers was listening to him, but not because they weren't interested, it was because they were all a little preoccupied thinking of their families and friends back home, and how they couldn't wait to see them all again, and how they just wanted to get back home to where they could once more feel safe, and hopefully could return to some sort of normality.

Dai was now flying over Merthyr Mountain at a height of 90 feet (27 metres) and everything was fine, no SAS had been waiting for them, because they hadn't been shot down shortly after take-off. However, neither Dai, or any of his passengers noticed a figure walking along the mountain with a high-powered hunting crossbow in his hand, and even if they had I doubt if they would have been too concerned, because they'd just think it was one of the locals out hunting rabbits to eat, and they would have been right.

No one would be expecting the person to take a potshot at the Chinook as it went overhead, (the person had led on his back to take the shot) and the reason he'd decided to do so was quite simply to see if he could hit it, never thinking for one moment that he'd actually manage it.

However just by pure chance the crossbow bolt with its aluminium shaft and stainless-steel arrowhead hit and pierced the fuel tank, this now posed a major problem for Dai as the warning lights started flashing telling him they were losing fuel, (the hunter had long gone) running as fast as he could once, he'd realized what he'd done, expecting a load of angry soldiers to be in hot pursuit at any moment.

Yet he was laughing his head off and couldn't wait to tell his friends how he'd shot a helicopter full of soldiers down with his crossbow, The hunters name was Dai Chard who is a local man from a small mining town called Bargoed which is in the Rhymney valley in South Wales. But no action was taken against him, except for a few of the local F T W supporters "having a word" if you know what I mean, once all the excitement had died down.

In the meantime, Dai Merlin Davies had managed to land safely on Bargoed mountain, he told Yikem and his associates to hide in the tall ferns until he returned, as he had to dispose of the Chinook as far away as possible, so he might not be back for several hours, Yikem agreed with Dai and told him to be careful, and not to take any risks, Dai just smiled and said I'll see you all in a bit, and with that he took off and was gone.

Now thankfully, Dai knew Bargoed mountain like the back of his hand as he'd spent a great deal of his youth up there before moving to Ireland, so he knew exactly where to ditch the Chinook, the awkward bit would be landing it, but he'd worry about that when he got there.

A few minutes later he was over a stretch of mountain between two villages one called Trelewis and the other called Bedlinog, where there was a narrow stretch of road that went up over the mountain, but it was very rarely used because it was a very narrow and twisty road along with the fact there was a sheer drop over the side and there were several burnt-out cars at the bottom of the drop to prove just how dangerous this stretch of road was.

Dai's plan was to land the Chinook in the ravine, where it would be very unlikely to be seen. The trick would be to land it without crashing, as there wasn't a lot of room for manoeuvring, and one slight mistake would be fatal, but Dai was fairly sure he could do it, so in he went.

Twenty minutes later Dai climbed out of his beloved Chinook, filled a bottle up with Aviation fluid said goodbye to her, and started the long hazardous climb up the ravine, once he'd made it up to the road, he took his RAF issue zippo lighter from his pocket, lit the makeshift fuse on his Aviation fluid bomb and threw it at the Chinook which then burst into flames.

Dai then started the long trek back to where Yikem and co were waiting, Yikem had seen the cloud of smoke that was now billowing up over the mountain, Eigroeg looked at him with a worried look on her face, and now they all thought that Dai had crashed and was either seriously injured, but more than likely dead.

Igoy immediately volunteered to go to the crash site to see if Dai was still alive, but both Yikem and Eigroeg said no, they would stay where they were until it was dark, the time was now 21.00 hours, they decided to wait until 23.00 hours and then Yikem and Igoy would go and have a look.

At 22.45 hours they heard a rustling sound coming towards them through the long ferns, there was a brief flash of light as someone quickly shone a torch as if trying to get their bearings, then they heard a familiar voice quietly saying Yikem where are you? It's me Dai.

It was just as well Dai spoke when he had, because Yikem, Igoy and two other members had quietly surrounded him, and were just about to pounce, but as soon as he spoke the four F T W members stood up scaring the life out of Dai who shouted, shit, you scared the life out of me, then, after a moments silence Dai realised what had nearly happened, and added (with a little chuckle in his voice) remind me to never upset you guys.

Yikem then explained how they'd seen the smoke rising and thought he'd crashed and was probably dead, Yikem then quickly added we were just about to come and look for you though, just in case you were alive but injured, Igoy then added I wanted to come and look for you as soon as we saw the smoke, but Yikem and Eigroeg said no we couldn't risk it.

Dai replied, they were right because that place will have quite a few people nosing around there for the next few days looking for anything that may be useful to them, but I doubt very much if it'll get reported to the authorities.

Our main priority now is finding somewhere safe for you all to stay, and I think I know just the place, it's no palace but if we can get in there, I know you'll be okay for a while, plus it's not that far from here I'd say a half an hour walk at the most.

Right then, said Dai, let's go, the sooner I get you guys somewhere safe the happier I'll be, and off they went. Dai was setting a good pace, whilst keeping close to the edge of the road so if they spotted any traffic heading towards them, they would have plenty of time to hide in the tall ferns and the darkness of the night.

True to his word half an hour later Dai stops, and says here we are then, but all the F T W could make out in the darkness was a small mound covered in grass about one-metre-high protruding out of the ground, and it had a two-metre-high fence around it and a metal gate that was secured by a rusty old lock that looked as if it had been on there for many decades and had seen better days.

Igoy then asked the question that the rest of the F T W was thinking, which was, so where's this hiding place then Dai? Dai laughed, and said it's here, your stood right next to it, and as he walked towards the gate, he said to Yikem, do you think you could get that lock of the gate as we don't have a key.

Yikem just grabbed the rusty old lock, and while still looking at Dai and with a smile on his face Yikem just pulled the lock and it came undone in his hand, much to Dai's delight which could be heard in his voice as he said oh! That'll do it then, as he realised, he could put the lock back on so it looked as if it was still locked, just in case anyone came looking for them in that area, because everything would appear as normal, and they wouldn't even think of trying the rusty old lock that looked seized solid and hadn't been touched for donkeys' years, so he knew the F T W would be safe until he could move them.

Then once they had managed to get the gate open which was no easy task as the hinges were rusted solid. Dai led the somewhat bewildered F T W through the gate and once everyone was through Dai took a bit of the chewing gum he had in his mouth and pushed it into the lock he then closed the gate and put the lock back where it belonged and pushed the shackle into the chewing gum thereby holding it in place and making it look as if the lock hadn't been touched.

Dai then jumped up on to the top of the mound, and as he said welcome to your new residence to the F T W, Dai went down on his hands and knees and started scrabbling about on the ground, and pulling large lumps of grass and soil out of the ground, after 10 minutes or so Dai said Yikem, could you give me a hand here please? A somewhat confused Yikem replied certainly, as he approached Dai, he noticed a large metal ring that was attached to what appeared to be some sort of manhole cover, Dai said to Yikem, could you please pull that metal ring? But please do it gently, to make sure it doesn't snap off. Yikem nodded and pulled the ring as gently as he could, eventually the "manhole cover opened with a loud creaking sound, Dai then said nice one, that hasn't been opened for a good twenty years at least. What at first glance appeared to be a manhole cover, was in fact a small, hinged metal door that once fully opened, revealed a set of steel ladder like steps leading down into a rather spacious room.

Once everyone was inside the "door" was closed and the handle had been turned thereby locking it, Dai shone his torch around to reveal several bunkbeds, and a decent sized table and chairs. The torch also revealed what appeared to be a light switch, which they tried, and much to everyone's amazement the light came on, now admittedly it wasn't the brightest light they'd ever seen, but it was more than adequate for what they needed.

Dai Merlin Davies then went on to explain that they were in an old air raid shelter left over from the second world war, and the reason the lights still worked was that they were twelve volts and ran off a large heavy duty leisure battery that was on constant charge thanks to the solar panel that was hidden in the top of a tree in the middle of a small area of woodland roughly one mile away, but even Dai had to admit he was as surprised as they were when the light turned on.

There was also a radio in there, (but they decided to leave that alone.) They even discovered a potbellied stove, complete with a small mountain of smokeless fuel, the stove also boasted built in carbon filters that guaranteed no smoke would come from the small chimney that barely rose above the ground several metres away from the shelter. They also found a cupboard full of rations, but they decided to leave them well alone, as there was plenty of food growing wild such as blackberries and Wimberries. Plus, there was a handful of allotments less than half a mile away if needed, so there was no chance of them going hungry.

But for now, all anybody wanted to do was sleep, so Dai had a quick rummage about for some bedding, and found a cupboard full of army sleeping bags, still sealed in the original wrapping...So, after a good eight hours sleep Dai told Yikem and Eigroeg how he had decided to take a walk into Bargoed town, which was only a few miles away, to see if anyone was talking about a helicopter crashing on Bedlinog mountain.

But everyone seemed to be carrying on as normal, so Dai thought he'd see if he could find any of the fifteen F T W supporters that lived in that area. Dai had photos of each member along with a list of names and addresses for them, (all which of course he had memorized) and as he walked around the town, he recognized two of them walking towards him, as they got closer Dai smiled at them said hello, and then said the password, so they'd know he was "safe" to talk too.

So, the F T W supporters whose names were Pat Ryder and her husband Craig Ryder replied with another code word, to verify who they were. Craig shook Dai's hand, then he said come with us, and we'll introduce you to the main man whose name was Arron (the Russian) Hughes. who runs the Macdonald Hotel in St Gwladys Avenue, so off they went to the pub, the introduction was made, they then went and sat in the lounge where it was quiet.

Dai started telling them everything that had happened, including the Helicopter crash, but they assured Dai that no one would say anything to the authorities about it, so he relaxed a bit after that, especially when they told him there would be nothing left of the helicopter after a few days or weeks at the most, as the locals would strip it down and weigh it in for food or items they needed at a "not too fussy" scrapyard that was owned by Clive (Bristler) Griffiths.

So now they got down to the business of getting another Helicopter, preferably a Puma, so the F T W could continue their journey home. And after several hours talking about various things, it was decided that a meeting of all fifteen F T W S would be arranged for the following evening. They would meet in the Lounge at The Macdonald Hotel at 19.00 hours, and with that Dai thanked them for their willingness to help, and how he was looking forward to meeting the others.

He said his goodbyes and left. He then went to tell the F T W what had happened. So as soon as Dai got back to the shelter, and making sure that no one was about, he undone the padlock on the gate, then quickly sealing it back up with more chewing gum, Dai then lifted the "hatch" and disappeared into the shelter, locking the hatch behind him.

He then proceeded to tell Yikem and co what had happened, and how there would be a meeting at 19.00 hours the next evening. He also explained how he didn't think they'd be staying in the air raid shelter for much longer, but he would know a lot more once the meeting was over.

This news made Yikem and associates a bit happier, as they were quite rightly starting to get a bit concerned, which is understandable considering nothing was going to plan, all thanks to a lucky or in their case an unlucky shot from a local hunter.

The next day seemed to drag, every hour seemed to take an age to pass, as Dai just wanted to get this meeting over and done with, so he could tell Yikem and his associates what had been planned.

Yikem, Eigroeg, and the rest of the F T W where also restless, Dai could see how they were becoming fed up with being cooped up in this shelter, and how they (understandably) just wanted to get back home to their friends, and family.

1800 hours finally arrived, and Dai was now beginning to get a bit restless, pacing around, deep in thought, he was also beginning to feel a bit anxious about this meeting, and was worrying in case no-one showed up, or maybe he'd be met by the police because it could all have been a set up.

He was also concerned that if the meeting did go ahead as planned whether they'd believe what he had to say, or would they just think he was some sort of nutter just spouting off, what if they wanted to meet Yikem and the other members of the F T W as proof of whether he was telling the truth or not.

Dai was now pacing up and down, like a father at the birth of his first child, which didn't go unnoticed in this small, confined space. Igoy was the first to ask Dai what was troubling him? Dai replied my heads gone into overload, and I'm beginning to think all sorts of things about the meeting.

Igoy replied, don't worry Dai you'll be fine, these people are on our side, and they want to help in any way they can, you're just working yourself up over nothing.

Eventually 18.30 had arrived, Dai was now ready to go to the meeting. He was just making sure he had the notes he'd prepared on questions to ask, and notes he'd prepared with answers to questions they may ask.

It was now 18.45, and he was finally ready, he was now feeling surprisingly calm and collected. As he made his way to the exit hatch every member of the F T W said good luck Dai, and we'll see you later. Dai just smiled and nodded his thank you to them all, then he was out of the hatch and gone.

Yikem, Eigroeg, Igoy and the others just sat there in the silence, staring at each other, and thinking to themselves, this is going to be a long night. Let's hope everything goes well.

As Dai walked in through the door of the McDonald Hotel, he noticed a sign on the lounge door stating the lounge was closed to the public due to a private function. Dai unknowingly gave out a sigh of relief as he realised the sign wouldn't be there if he'd been set up.

He gingerly opened the lounge door and walked in. There were roughly thirty people sat in there quite happily chatting away too each other, as they waited for Dai to arrive.

Every one of them stopped talking as soon as he walked through the door, they just sat there in silence, staring at the stranger that had just casually strolled in. After a few awkward seconds, that seemed like hours. Craig and pat Ryder came through the door leading from the bar.

They walked over to Dai with big smiles on their faces, both shook his hand vigorously, they then turned to face the other members of the F T W S and said (rather proudly) right then you lot, this is Dai that I told you about, please make him feel welcome and at home.

As Dai, Craig and Pat walked towards their seats everyone they passed said hello, pleased to meet you. Once they'd sat down Craig asked Dai if he'd like a drink? Dai replied I'll have a pint of bitter please, everyone in the room said, oh, cheers Craig, I'll have a pint as well if you're offering, nice one butty, to which he replied, yeah, right, and you all know what you can do and all. Everyone went, oh well, it was worth a go, and they all started laughing loudly. Dai just sat there smiling, and thinking to himself, brilliant, I'm sat in a pub full of nutters, but good nutters if you know what I mean.

Craig returned from the bar with the drinks (this pub brewed their own beer and the regulars paid for it by bartering goods, for example many of them had allotments and they grew the hops needed to make the beer, others provided logs for the fires etc.) Then the introductions started. Once that was done and everyone had finally settled down, Craig went to the bar and called Aaron (the Russian) to come and join them.

Everyone else in the pub just thought it was another private party and just carried on as normal. Russian told the other two bartenders that he would look after the lounge bar, so there was no need for them to come in there, and how he didn't want to be disturbed for any reason.

His staff replied okay boss, and off they went. Russian then joined the crowd in the lounge and officially declared that the meeting was now in progress. He introduced Patricia Ryder to Dai by saying this is Pat, and if it's okay with you she'll be responsible for keeping the minutes, which of course you'll have a copy of once the meeting is finished. Dai replied yep, that's fine, and we've already met, he then shook Pat's hand, smiled, and nodded his head towards her in acknowledgement. Pat smiled and nodded back she then sat next to Dai and Aaron the Russian. The meeting was now officially underway.

Everyone then (rather excitedly) started asking Dai all sorts of questions, but they were all asking them at the same time. Russian stood up, told everyone to shut up, and then told them if anyone had a question, they should raise their hand and wait until it was their turn.

A voice that belonged to Dai (evs) Evans, was heard at the back commenting, that it was like being back in school. Russian looked at him, and said Dai evs, how the hell would you know? You were never there. Everyone thought it was highly amusing when Dai evs (whilst looking at the floor in mock embarrassment) replied, well I must admit you're not wrong on that one butty.

Russian then asked if anyone had a better idea?

There were no replies, and every hand in the room shot up into the air. Russian then pointed at one member named Craig Ryder, (Pat's husband) and said right then Craig, what's your question? Craig then looked straight at Dai, smiled, nodded, and said hello Dai, it's a pleasure to meet you again, and I'm sure I speak for everyone here when I say, we will do whatever it takes to help you in any way we can.

We may not look much, and there's not that many of us, but believe me, we are a very "resourceful" bunch here in the valley's if you catch my drift. He then went on to say how people are fed-up with not having any gas or electricity for cooking, heating, and light, luckily most people in this area still have open fireplaces, so they do all the cooking, and for boiling the water from the local river etc. on them, but we are cutting trees down for firewood, which obviously isn't good for the environment, and to be honest it's a real pain in the arse. So how do you intend to solve this problem?

Dai smiled and nodded at Craig and replied, now that's a good question. What we intend to do is put solar panels on every household, factory, and shop, to provide free renewable energy. This will happen once the solar panel manufacturing gets underway. Many are already up and are now running none stop, twenty-four hours a day, seven days a week. Many other premises are being repaired because they were wrecked by senseless looters. So, I'll be asking for volunteers to help in any way they can, so if you have any skills that could be useful, please let me know later on as we would train you in how to make the solar panels. We also intend to show you how to make a copy of a generator that was invented by a man named Tessla, but we have simplified it. What we do is modify the portable petrol/diesel generators.

We remove the now useless engines, and we replace them with a wheel that have magnets attached to the inside, to spin the wheel, thereby generating electricity. In other words, we use the magnets instead of the original engine, and believe it or not, it works. You can also run your petrol generator on a thing called a Hydrogen cell, which basically is a container full of saltwater, and a 12volt car battery.

I'll quite happily show anyone that's interested how to do these things, we are also in the process of drawing up plans to show people how to do it.

So basically, the petrol run generators will use Hydrogen cells, and the Diesel ones will run off magnets. But of course, both types of generators will run on magnets, it's up to the individual which type they'd prefer, but personally I'd recommend using magnets because once it's up and running then that's it, whereas the Hydrogen cell will need topping up with saltwater which is a bit scarce at the moment, but we intend to sort that out very soon.

There are loads of these generators lying around abandoned because people believe they're no good anymore. So, if you know or see any of them, then grab them and we'll convert them. Craig replied, sounds good. But how long is it going to take to get it all setup?

Dai replied, I must admit it's not going to happen overnight, and that's why we'd like to teach you how to convert them yourselves, then you can train others to do it, and you'll be surprised just how quickly it'll take off. The only problem we can see is once all the portable generators are being used it could lead to people trying to steal someone else's.

However, we have our Boffins (for want of a better word) working on it as we speak, they have already created a generator that's roughly the size of a domestic microwave, that runs completely silent, it can provide more than enough electricity to run a four-bedroomed house.

We're trying to get production up and running as soon as possible. Craig replied, well like I said earlier, we'll do everything we can to help to get things back to normal. Russian then pointed at another man and said, go on then Jeff, what's your question? Jeff then said, hello Dai, my name is Jeff Weaver, and my question is this. The generator conversions you mentioned earlier; can you do this to any generator? For example, the big generators in shipping containers like the ones they use on Building sites etc., could you convert them?

Dai replied, hello Jeff, I'm very pleased to meet you, and yes, we can. Not only that, but the diesel generators would be silent running, so as I mentioned earlier, you wouldn't even know it was running. The hardest part would be transporting them to where they are needed. And obviously the big ones would be used to power hospitals and factories etc.

Jeff just smiled and said, oh, I think we could sort something out (jeff was a local coalman and had two big lorries that could carry the big generators.) He then said thanks Dai, that's handy to know, because I know where there's two of them not all that far from here. Dai replied, brilliant Jeff, we can have a chat about them a bit later on, once I've (hopefully) answered everyone's questions.

Jeff replied (with a smile on his face) well, you'd best get comfy then, it looks like it's going to be a long old night. Dai looked around and every person in the room had their hands in the air. Including the ones stood by the bar, Aaron the Russian (who was trying to serve them as quickly as he could) told them to put their hands down until they were sat down.

Eventually everyone was back in their seats and much to everyone's disappointment Aaron told them the bar was now closed until the end of the meeting, because it was causing too much disruption.

(Plus, he was fed up with going back and forth to the bar every couple of minutes like a blue arsed fly) he then said, if the bar is closed then the meeting shouldn't take too long. So, with that thought in mind let's get on with it shall we? He then said right then Stephen Gant lets have your question please. Stephen replied, thank you. He then said hello Dai, I'm very pleased to meet you, and I hope you can answer this question for me, as a lot of people are really quite concerned over some of the rumours that are going around about how the F T W intend to use people as slaves, or pets, and/or breeding us for food. The room fell silent, everyone in the room was now watching Dai intently. Dai just smiled and said, please, believe me when I say all these rumours are just that, rumours, put out by the government to scare people. If you think about it, if there was any truth in them then we wouldn't be sat here having this meeting, and I certainly wouldn't be sat here representing them, as like many of you I have a family of my own, and like yourselves I want them to have a future. We have abused this planet for far too long. It's time to put things right, everyone applauded Dai's comment. Stephen Gant said thankyou Dai, that's exactly what I was hoping you'd say. Aaron then said right Geraint Rowlands lets have your question please, Geraint said hello

Dai, can you explain how the animals and insects became self-aware, and how did they become so intelligent so quickly? And are the rumours true that they can talk to each other? Dai replied, well, that's a good question. Unfortunately, I can only partially answer it, as I honestly have no idea how it all came about. But I can tell you that yes, they can talk to each other, and many of them can also understand, and speak to us, they can also speak every language in the world.

There was complete silence for a few minutes, until Kerry Wilkins said, wow, now that wasn't the answer we expected. So, will we get to meet any of the talking ones? Not that I'm calling you a liar, but you must admit it does sound a bit farfetched.

Dai replied, I will do my best to get in touch with the F T W and see if I can arrange something, but of course the main priority would have to be their safety, but I promise I'll do my best. The meeting went on for another four hours before Aaron the Russian said, right I think that's about covered everything, so if there's no more questions, I'll open the bar.

While everyone was getting their drinks, Dai was sat talking to a man named Dorian Griffiths, Dai said to him, hopefully we can start teaching everyone how to convert the generators, my main problem at the moment is I need another helicopter, and I need it as soon as possible. Dorian replied, I'll be back in a minute, he then stood up and walked over to another table where three men were sat talking, Dorian sat down and started talking to them and pointed at Dai, the three men nodded in agreement and Dorian called him over to join them.

Once he had joined them Dorian introduced him to the men. They were Dorians brothers, Mark, Clive, and Keith. Dorian explained to

Dai how he and his brothers may be able to help with the helicopter problem and was there any particular helicopter he had in mind? as they knew a place that had quite a few different types. The place they mentioned with the helicopters wasn't that far from Bargoed. It was just over the Severn bridge it was a top-secret airbase which was disguised as a museum. All the exhibits were in good working order. Dorians brother Clive knew one of the security guards that works the nightshift there, Clive said he would have a word with him to see what could be done about "acquiring" one, preferably a Puma.

So, a few days later a trip to the base was arranged. Clive, his family, and Dai would go there as visitors, so Dai could see exactly what was there, and which ones were available to "acquire" without too many problems. Plus, the F T W new the base had a good stock of aviation fuel, the F T W had let them keep it for displays, and helicopter rides for the "paying" customers. Plus, the fuel and all flights were being closely monitored by the F T W. So, the visit was done.

A fully functioning Puma Helicopter was discovered, Contact was made with the security guard whose name was Saul Oakey. A plan was formed as to how and when the Puma could be "acquired" as Saul had told them how there was an open day planned for the 29th of August, which was two weeks away, which Dai thought that would be enough time to get things organised, he promised Saul that he'd be in touch within the next couple of days to confirm whether the plan was ready or not.

Dai Beeza Merlin Davies thanked Saul for his time and once again told him he would be back to see him within two days, he then shook his hand, thanked him again, and Clive, his family and Dai left. Dai just wanted to get back to the air raid shelter to tell Yikem Snave and co exactly what had happened and how (hopefully) they would all be on their way home within the next two weeks. After what seemed a lifetime, they eventually made it back to Bargoed. Clive took his family home and then gave Dai a lift back to the pub, Clive returned home, and Dai headed for the Air raid shelter. Eager to share the good news, and to start working out how he was going to get Yikem and co to Bristol without being seen, and then getting them aboard the Puma, again without being seen. He reckoned Saul Oakey's local knowledge would be very useful in resolving this problem. He eventually arrives at the shelter, and after checking no-one was around, he slipped the lock off the gate then resealed it with chewing gum, he quickly lifted the hatch and entered the shelter. Yikem and co could tell just by the look on his face that everything went well.

Igoy was the first of the F T W to ask how did you get on? Dai sat down next to him with a big smile on his face as he said, all went really well. He then went on to tell them in great detail exactly what went had happened, and how they had a fully functioning Puma, just sat there waiting to be used. He also told them of the aviation fuel store that was adequately stocked. He then went on to explain how the security guard was more than willing to help them "acquire" the fully fueled Puma and how the museum had an open day planned for the 29th of August, so they had two weeks to come up with a workable plan. Dai then explained how he had told the security guard, Saul how he would go back in two days' time to confirm that they would be ready to leave on the 28th. Every member of the F T W let out a big sigh of relief, knowing that they could be back with their family and friends in the not-too-distant future.

They also knew they were taking a big risk to achieve their goal; they also knew that they really didn't have much if any choice, they had to go for it, shit or bust. So, they immediately started to work on the plan, Igoy was already in touch with Ycnan and Haras Snave, and within minutes they had the basis of a good, workable, plan in place, it just needed a little tweaking and refining, such as how they were going to get the F T W to the air base without being seen. Plus, they had to get them into the Helicopter without being seen. But to be honest it shouldn't be too difficult, but everything had to be meticulously planned, like a military operation. Which of course the F T W were more than capable of doing. It was now 19.00 hours, by 03.00 hours the plan was a good as completed, just needed to have the final read through by Ycnan and Haras Snave, Dai Beeza Merlin Davies had been busy getting transport arranged, and he was also busy sorting out a meeting between some of the more trusted members of the F T W S and a few selected members of the F T W. Igoy had already volunteered to attend the meeting, and although Ycnan and Haras Snave weren't too happy about it Yikem had already told everyone that he was going, as he wanted to meet, and personally thank the supporters for everything they had done, as without their help this escape plan would never have been put together.

It was now 0.700 hours, everyone in the shelter was exhausted. 07.30 hours, every one of them was fast asleep. Safe in the knowledge this plan had covered every scenario that could possibly happen, they had a 98% chance of everything going to plan. So, the 25th of August arrives. The plan has been double checked and re-checked several times, just to make sure. The planned route and the "backup" routes had undergone the same checks. The transport was all sorted. All was good.

They were now ready to go on the 28th. Understandably the F T W ambassadors were excited and worried at the thought of it all. They knew this would be their only chance of making it home. On the 27th the meeting between the F T W and a selected number of supporters took place. The meeting was held in the back of a long wheelbase van that was parked out of sight, behind the underground reservoir buildings which was roughly 100 yards away from the Air raid shelter. (Although the supporters had no idea that the F T W were in there.) At 19.00 hours Dai Beeza Merlin Davies, along with Yikem Snave and Igoy arrived at the van. Jeff Weaver who was sat in the driver's seat jumped out and quickly opened the side door so they could get in. Sat inside waiting were, Aaron (The Russian), Keri Wilkins, along with Craig and Pat Ryder.

Every one of them just sat there staring not knowing what to say to these two huge mountain gorillas that had just climbed in. Keri Wilkins was the first to speak he said, hello, how are you, my name is Keri, as he spoke, he stood up with his hand outstretched to shake hands with them. Igoy automatically stepped forward to shake Keri's hand. (and to shield Yikem Snave in case of any "problems") when Igoy shook his hand he said, hello Keri my name is Igoy, it's a pleasure to meet you and your friends, all the supporters just looked at each other with big silly grins on their faces, Keri responded with, bloody hell, we all knew you could talk, but it's still come as a bit of a shock, then quickly added no offence meant. Both Igoy and Yikem laughed and said, it's okay, and no offence taken. Igoy then introduced Yikem Snave to them all, and in turn they all shook hands and introduced themselves. Eventually after a few minutes when everyone had calmed down and relaxed the conversation started with Yikem walking over to Craig and Pat Ryder and said, I would like to thank you and your colleagues for everything you've done to help us, he then turned to Aaron, and I'd like to thank you for putting this team of supporters together. Without you and your team this escape plan would never have happened.

Aaron replied, it's our pleasure to help you, we just want things to get back to some kind of normality, so we can hopefully all live together peacefully. The plan and route to get the F T W to Weston super mare was explained to Jeff Weaver who would be driving the van and Keri Wilkins who would be "co-pilot" and backup driver just in case anything happened to Jeff. The meeting ended at 22.00 hours. Everyone said goodbye, and good luck to Igoy and Yikem. Jeff and Keri said, we'll see you tomorrow night, at 15.30 hours already for the off. It would take roughly one hour to get to the air base, which meant they would arrive on the outskirts half an hour before it closed to the public, plus Saul Oakey would be starting his security duty at 17.00, so they'd be able to meet him just before the start of his shift, just to double check that the Puma was fully fueled, checked, and ready to go.

They had arranged to meet the security guard Saul Oakey in the big layby just down the road from the air base. They arrived at the layby at 16.30, and sure enough Saul was there waiting for them. They had a quick chat where Saul confirmed everything had been checked and fully fueled ready to go. They told him they would be on site at 22.30 and intended to leave at 23.00 at the latest.

Saul agreed that would be the best time, he then shook hands with Dai Beeza Merlin Davies, and left. So, they now had a few hours to kill, but decided to stay where they were, the last thing they wanted to do was draw attention to the van. Eventually 22.30 arrived, everyone was on edge, hoping that everything would go to plan. Jeff Weaver started the van, then looking around the van, he asks, is everyone okay? They all nodded yes, not a single one of them spoke. Jeff then said, okey dokey, here we go, it'll all be okay, stop worrying. Two minutes later they were at the air base gates, Saul Oakey was there waiting for them, as he saw them approaching, he opened the gates so they could drive straight in, he pointed them in the direction he wanted them to go, then closed the gates and walked over to where they were parked, engine and lights were turned off.

Dai Beeza Merlin Davies was the first one out of the van, Saul said, hello Dai, everything is ready for you, all fueled up, and ready to go, everything has been checked, but I dare say you'll want to do your own checks, which is fine, because as you run your checklist, I'll get your passengers aboard. Dai nodded in agreement, then turned and started to walk the 100 yards (91.44 metres) to the helicopter, Yikem and Eigroeg Snave, along with the rest of the F T W representatives were saying goodbye, and thankyou to Jeff and Keri.

They then turned and quickly walked to the helicopter, Dai was already doing his preliminary checks as they got in, Saul showed them to their seats and started to show them how to use the seatbelts, Yikem smiled at Saul and said, thankyou Saul, but we know how the belts work, as we used them on the flight here.

Saul started to apologize but Yikem cut him short by grabbing his hand and started shaking it as he said, thank you for all your help, it won't be forgotten, and if we can ever help you in anyway then please don't hesitate to ask. Saul, somewhat confused said thank you, but how would I contact you? At that point Dai said, right then, checks done, are we all okay to go? Yikem just smiled and said to Saul, don't worry about it, we'll know. Jeff or Keri will explain it to you when we have left. And thank you once again for your help.

Yikem, Eigroeg, Igoy, and the remaining five ambassadors whose names were, Daic, Anetha, Eboehp, Griac, and Ymmat, turned to Dai and said, we are all strapped in ready to go. Saul climbed out of the helicopter, wished them all good luck, and retreated to a safe distance. They took off, Saul, Jeff and Keri stood there and watched them disappear into the night, Keri said to Saul, I really hope they make it safely back home, Jeff and Saul nodded in agreement.

Well, said Keri, it must be time to tie you up then? So as to give you an alibi. Saul smiled and said okay, let's get this over with, the three of them walked into the reception area of the base, sat Saul down in a chair and tied his wrists to the arms of the chair with some cable ties, they cable tied his ankles to the base of the chair, sat facing the office desk, they didn't bother to gag him as there was no need as no-one would hear him scream, (which he had no intention of doing) Jeff asked if he was okay? Cable ties not too tight? Saul replied no I'm fine, let's hope I don't need the toilet, but I should be okay as they normally start coming in to work around 0.500 hours. (It was now0.100 hours.) Keri (with a big smile on his face) said to Saul, do you want the telly on? I'll put the remote control in your hand if you want. Saul replied, naah, best not, it'd look a bit obvious, wouldn't it? So, Jeff and Keri said, well, that's it then, we hope you don't get into too much trouble over this. Oh. By the way, the F T W where serious when they said if they can ever help you, they would. All you'd have to do is mention it to any animal or insect and it'll be done. To be honest with you I think they'll be watching you, just to make sure you are okay. Anyway, we'd better go as we've got to get back home yet. Thanks again Saul, and take care my friend, we'll pop over to see you in a few weeks to see if you're okay. We'll shut the doors on the way out. And with that, they were out the door, and gone. Meanwhile the helicopter, which was now over the ocean heading for Portugal, the mood had lightened considerably, thanks to Igoy, who had broken the ice by asking what time the inflight film would be starting? Then. (Jokingly) added, I Hope it's not The Fugitive, or The Great Escape. and what time would the hostess be around with the snacks and drinks? Which made everyone laugh.

Meanwhile, back in Builth Wells, Colonel Glyn Adams was rather busy. (In order to keep up the pretence that the F T W were still there) he was telling the Prime Minister how, over the last few weeks he had slowly but surely made some progress in reaching an agreement with the F T W, as they had finally agreed to alter some of their demands in order to help find a compromise to get an agreement signed between them and the governments of this world.

However, the F T W had pointed out on several occasions how the World Governments had refused to alter their demands. If anything, their demands had increased. So, the F T W had written a list of these demands that had to be altered, or preferably revoked, in order for progress to be made. The Prime Minister, who was now at his wits ends after several weeks of very little sleep, thanks to the fire ant's presence in number 10, was now more than willing to do whatever it took to get this agreement settled. He then told Colonel Adams how he would talk to the World Leaders to agree with whatever the F T W wanted in order to get it done.

But of course, the agreement wouldn't be worth the paper it was written on. It was just a ploy to lead the F T W into a false sense of security, giving mankind a chance to regroup and to come up with a plan to "take back" what was rightfully theirs.

Colonel Adams advised the Prime Minister how that wouldn't be a good idea, as the F T W always seemed to know what our plans are. The Prime Minister replied, I really don't give a shit what you, or anybody else think, that's why I run this country and you are just a soldier that does what he's told.

Colonel Adams replied, yeah right, and look at the state of things at the moment, you arrogant fool, and before you come out with the usual excuse of, these circumstances where beyond our control, just let me remind you how experts have been saying for decades how we need to look after this planet or face the consequences. The Prime Minister angrily replied. You do your job and I'll do mine. Colonel Adams replied I'm doing my job and yours, I'm the one that has to face them every day, while you sit safely tucked up in your home, complaining about the "hardships" you and your family are suffering, while the majority of people, including families with young children, are living on the streets, struggling to survive on a daily basis. You are an arsehole. You genuinely have no idea of what's going on in the real world. And what really pisses me off is the fact that you don't want to know.

As usual the Prime Minister got on his high horse and started ranting, do you know who you are talking too? You will treat me with respect or lose your job. You are nothing more than cannon fodder, and easily replaced. Colonel Adams replied, I tell you what, you are an arrogant, pompous twat, you can shove your job up your arse. I resign, as of now I am a civilian.

The Prime Minister said, how dare you speak to me like that, I refuse to accept your resignation. Colonel Adams replied, tough shit, I'm leaving, right now, find yourself another whipping boy. The Prime

Minister responded with; I'll have you shot for dereliction of duty and deserting your post. Colonel Adams replied, how are you going to do that then? Being as you have nothing to shoot me with, goodbye. I'm leaving. And with that the Colonel put the phone down, collected all his stuff, he handed his security pass over to the sergeant, told him that he was now in charge until his replacement arrived, and left.

The Prime Minister was furious and called for his personal secretary to get in touch with the minister in charge of the armed forces in order to get a replacement for Colonel Adams sent to Builth Wells immediately, and to make sure the replacement had been fully briefed in all aspects of what was going on there.

In the meantime, the F T W had safely landed in a private airfield in Portugal. The helicopter was quickly placed in a hanger, so it was out of sight. Yikem and associates were escorted from the helicopter into another room where they could have something to eat and rest, while the Puma was refueled and all safety checks were carried out to ascertain whether the Puma could continue the journey to Algeria and then on to their final destination, which was Niger.

Where transport would be waiting for them to finally take them home to their family and friends.

Yikem and Co were busy feeding themselves as they were famished, and shortly after they all fell asleep safe in the knowledge that everything was fine. Eight hours later Yikem was woken up by Dai Beeza Merlin Davies gently nudging him whilst saying Yikem, wake up, its nearly time to leave. Yikem slowly came around, finally he was wide awake and started waking the others, whilst asking Dai how long have, we been asleep? Dai replied at least eight hours.

I myself haven't been awake for long. Our hosts came and woke me about fifteen minutes ago to tell me that the Puma was now fully fueled, all the maintenance checks had been done, and everything is fine, so if it's okay with you I'll start the preflight checks and we can be on our way. Yikem replied, yes that's fine Dai, and thank you. Dai replied, oh! don't thank me yet my friend, you're not home yet. Although I can't really see any problems from here on in, but as the old saying goes, never count your chickens until they hatch.

Which by the look on Yikem's face had confused him? So, Dai explained what it meant, to which Yikem replied, no offence Dai but you humans have some weird quirks don't you. Especially in what you laughingly call "the educated world" where you worship gods that you cannot see. And each religion preaches peace yet none of them will ever achieve it because they are too busy fighting amongst themselves to prove which god is the true god. Yet you fail to see that mother nature is the true creator and you are quite happy to destroy all of mother nature's creations, including what you need to survive on this planet solely for profit. Your population continually rises, yet you still carry on with the senseless destruction while you vainly. Proclaim yourselves as the most intelligent animal on the planet.

You have introduced your "educated world" to the jungle tribes that were quite happily living their lives and only taking what the needed, and you have now turned them into murderers, that kill the wildlife such as tigers, rhinos and elephants to earn a pittance from you for the ivory, rhino horn and tiger bones, while you make huge profits while they take the risks. We call it "the white man's disease" simply because whatever you touch you destroy. And that's why we are in this situation. Humans have no respect for what's around them. They don't even respect themselves. You build an artificial world to live in never thinking about the damage you are doing to the natural habitat and its inhabitants. Thankfully not all humans think this way. Yet your species is quick to ridicule the very people that are trying to help you.

You call them conspiracy theorists, tree huggers, etc. and that's why we finally had to step in and take control over you because you will not face the fact that you are slowly killing yourselves, and more importantly you are killing all life on this planet. Humans will eventually destroy themselves, fine, carry on, that's your choice. But all the other lifeforms don't deserve to die because of your incompetence and greed.

Dai was shocked by what Yikem had said, but he had to concede that Yikem was absolutely right in what he'd said. He then asked Yikem what did he suggest humans should do to rectify the problem? Yikem replied, it's quite simple really, stop living in a throwaway society, and learn to respect the planet. Yikem then went on to explain that all life on this planet is inextricably linked, and if you interfere with one link it will then have a knock-on effect to all the other links. Humans are not the most needed lifeform on this planet. In truth the lower down the food chain the more important they are. So, the most important life form is the algae that live under the Arctic ice, because they are the beginning of the food chain, without them life cannot exist.

I could go on, but we'd be here a very long time, so we'll continue this conversation another time. Dai agreed, and said, I look forward to it, and with that they walked off together to tell the others that it was time to leave for the final leg of their journey home. So, Dai started the preflight checks while Yikem got the rest of the F T W representatives into the Puma, ready to go.

Yikem thanked the people in charge of the airfield for all their help and he climbed into the Puma and said, okay Dai, let's go home. Dai replied, (jokingly) certainly sir. Your wish is my command.

Everyone smiled and nodded to the airfield crew. And away they went. Everyone was now in high spirits and were all excited about finally making it back home to their loved ones and friends. Four hours later and their journey was over. Dai landed the Puma in a clearing on the Chad/Niger border where they were met by some F T W supporters in a big troop transporter lorry. All the F T W delegates said thankyou to dai for getting them all home safely, Yikem shook his hand vigorously as he thanked him, and asked him what he intended to do now?

Yikem told him he would be more than welcome to stay with them for as long as he liked. Dai replied. That's very kind of you, but I'd best get back home, or they'll be wondering where the hell I am. I have planned for refueling on the way home so I should be okay. I have enough fuel to get me back to the airfield we left. So, I can't see any problems.

Well, Yikem my friend it seems my mission is over. So, I'll say goodbye for now. Please say goodbye to your associates and your sister for me please. And with that Dai jumped back into the Puma and was just about to start it up ready to go when Yikem came running over to him shouting dai, dai. I've just been told that the world Governments have all agreed to our demands. It's over dai. It's all over... We've won.

Dai replied well done, thank God for that. Hopefully now we can get back to some normality. But if you ever need me again for anything you know where I am. I haven't forgotten the conversation we had earlier about how we need to change the way humans look at this world. And I will do my best to do what you suggested. And once more congratulations to you and your fellow F T W members.

Yikem told dai that nothing would change in the next few months as the F T W would be having meetings with the world governments to finalise the agreements that will be drawn up. And with that dai once more said his goodbyes, waited for Yikem to get to a safe distance from the Puma and off he went on his journey home. Dai had plenty of time to ponder over what he'd been told on his long flight home.

And he thought to himself well, so it seems we will now live in a world without wars, without weapons and with more consideration for what we do to each other and the planet. Sounds lovely, if it happens, but I can't see the big arms manufacturers accepting this.

But then again, they have no other choice, they have to accept what has happened. But I really don't think it'll be as easy as that. I think the F T W will still have a long battle ahead of them. But I am certain of one thing. And that is, the F T W will not backdown. They hold all the cards in this game. And they are determined to win. Good luck to them. I will back them one hundred percent.

This has certainly opened my eyes to the way the human world works. Profit for big companies by destroying the planet is just madness. But sadly, it's all they think about. Hopefully now things will change for the better, putting everything that lives on this planet before profit would be a great start. And I sincerely hope it will eventually be accepted by everyone.

The F T W have proven without a shadow of a doubt that we don't need to use fossil fuels, the world produces more than enough energy than we could ever use on a daily basis. We just need to harness it with solar panels, wind and or water turbines. Etc. and I dare say over time we will create new and better ways to harness this unending source of energy. And I wish them nothing but luck in their attempts to create a better cleaner world for us, our children, and their children. It definitely gives us a goal to aim for. And I do believe that the world governments will be shocked at just how many people will back the F T W in all their endeavors. But for now, all we can do is sit back and wait for the outcome of the meetings between the governments and the F T W. we can but hope that all goes well. But as I said earlier, I don't think it's over yet by any means. But as I said we can only hope and give support to the F T W.

Oh! And if you are wondering what happened to colonel Glyn Adams. He resigned from the military and became a best-selling Author after publishing his book, corruption in the world governments. And on the proceeds of this book, he setup an agency investigating corruption in big companies, including certain branches of government.

He's doing really well. And has publicly announced his allegiance to the F T W. So.it would appear we are going to share and live peacefully together on this planet. However, the thing on everyone's mind (both human and animal) is how long this peace will last? Because we all know just how devious mankind can be. So, the F.T.W will be monitoring them very closely for many years to come.

There is one thing that mankind needs to keep in the back of their mind, and that is, the next time you decide to stamp on a spider, or swat a fly, just remember one vital thing.

We know where you live.